TWOC

Graham Joyce is the author of nine adult novels and has won numerous awards for his writing, including four British Fantasy Awards and the 2003 World Fantasy Award for *The Facts of Life*. Among his previous jobs he has been a teacher and spent eight years working for a youth organisation. Graham Joyce currently teaches creative writing at Nottingham Trent University and lives in Leicester with his wife and two children.

Praise for Graham Joyce's writing:

'I have not been so charmed by a novel in a long time.'
Isabel Allende on *The Facts of Life*

'You don't merely read a Graham Joyce novel, you live through it.' *SFX*

'An author in full command of his considerable talents.'
The Times

'Graham Joyce writes the kind of novels we keep hoping to find, but rarely do.' Jonathan Carroll

GRAHAM Joyce

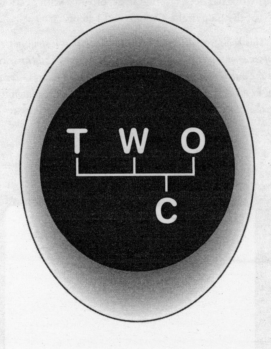

ff

faber and faber

First published in 2005
by Faber and Faber Limited
3 Queen Square London WCIN 3AU

Typeset by Faber and Faber Ltd
Printed in England by Mackays of Chatham plc, Chatham, Kent

A CIP record for this book
is available from the British Library

ISBN 0–571–22513–6

2 4 6 8 10 9 7 5 3 1

To Michael Joyce
and to Stephen Joyce.
Pack your own lunch, boys.

TWOC (twok) abbr. of criminal offence of Taking Without Owner's Consent as distinct from Theft, usually applied to motoring offence of so-called 'joyriding'.

Do We Have to Have It So Loud?

He's out there.

He's always out there. I crank up the volume on my CD so I can't hear him tapping on the window. That's one thing about Jake: all this tapping and scratching on the glass is weak, feeble even, so I can blast it out of all hearing just by toggling the volume. Plus, I know the old man won't bang on the door and go 'For Jesus' Sake Matt Do You Have To Have It So Freaking Loud?' Mum too. They know I'm in, at least. It means they know I'm here.

I think about rolling a spliff just to keep my thoughts off Jake. Just a little one. Though that might have Dad knocking on the door and going, 'Jake! What's That Funny Smell?'

Since it happened, Dad talks to me using initial capital letters. You might have noticed. He also speaks kind of slow, with each word carefully chosen. 'Think Hard Matt. Is This Really What You Want To Do With Your Life?' Or, my personal favourite, 'Can We Talk About This?' To which I reply, 'Right, Dad.' But I don't want to get caught with a spliff and I can't open the window to blow out the smoke because that's where Jake is. Though I don't look in Jake's direction, because it only encourages him. And it kind of enrages him, too.

Instead I sink my head into *Gravity Drop!* on the PlayStation. I'm pretty cool with it, level eight (sorta), and the game makes plenty of funky brain-mashing noises so I can completely blank Jake at the window. My bedroom is a techno-cave. Somehow my punishment for what happened was to be bought anything I asked for. I have a hi-fi, plasma-screen computer, keyboards so hot my fingers are smokin', games, MP3, WAP phone, DVD and about a hundred yards of cable writhing in the corner like a nest of black adders. I'm Hardware Harry. I'm Software Sam. I'm Download Dave.

Since it happened I don't care who I am.

But it doesn't matter what I do, or how loud I crank up the volume, or how deep into level eight I swim in *Gravity Drop!* I just can't help myself. It's like trying to keep your hands off yourself when you're between the sheets at night and thinking about Debbie Summerhill nude. Your hands just move to the spot like they're magnetised, programmed.

And in the same way my eyes move and I have to look at Jake. It's almost as if it were Debbie at the window, and not Jake at all: as if she were naked, waving behind the glass and scratching to get in to climb all over me. So I steal a look. I can't help myself. Just a flicker as my eye moves away from the whirling mousehole in *Gravity Drop!* Just a tiny flicker.

Sideways, to the window, and he's caught me, and I'm hooked like a harbour crab on a kid's line, with only the weight of my hatred pulling me back into the blue.

So I give up and look Jake straight in the eye. He gives a very tiny grin as he sees he's got me. I think it's a grin. His mouth is distorted because it's stuck up against the window, his lips mashed against the glass, dribbling a little, like a slug's trail. In fact, that's how he hangs there, using his mouth as a kind of sucker. He's showing off as he performs a 'Look, no hands' routine for me, flapping his arms through the air, held aloft only by the suction of his lips on the glass.

It's not a bad trick. Considering. Considering we're on the twelfth floor, that is.

I could just open the window and shake him off. I know he'd fall away and flutter to the ground like a leaf, but he'd be back in an hour. He's always back in an hour. So I just look at him with what I imagine to be an expression of contempt. But again I can't help myself. I go right up to the window and I say, loud enough for him to hear above the music and the idling prompt of the game, 'Jake, just what the fuck are you wearing?'

Next day, Sarah regards me steadily. I think it's a ruse. I think she's run out of ideas, blinking at me like that. Like she wants me to believe she's thinking deep stuff, but in fact it's all beyond her. Why wouldn't it be? I'm beyond myself now.

3

'Is he still dressing up?' she wants to know.

'Yeh. He was like a Turkish pickpocket or something.'

She shakes her head a little. I call it the gnat-flick. Like there's a summer gnat flitting by her eyebrow and she's trying to shake it away. 'Oh? And what does a Turkish pickpocket look like?'

The note in her voice makes me cagey. One time I explained that Jake came as a Scottish card-cheat and she went all serious on me and told me she was half-Scottish and did I realise my prejudices? 'Och aye, lass,' I said, but she didn't find that funny. In fact she freaked out. And here we are again. I admit it's not great for Turkish pickpockets that Jake is hanging on to windows by his lips, passing himself off as one, but what am I supposed to do about that? It's not as if I tell Jake what to wear, is it? I don't dress him. I'm not his makeover artist, or his personal valet. 'He wore a curly turban.'

She raises one eyebrow. 'A *curly* turban?'

'Yeh, not like one that the Sikhs wear, but, you know, it winds round, like with those genies in *Aladdin*. And his shoes were curled up at the toes.'

'Aladdin was Chinese. Not Turkish.'

'I can't help that! I can't help it if Jake comes in a turban, or if he's Turkish or whatever! What's that got to do with me if he comes as a Turkish pickpocket or as a Chinese one?'

'Calm down, Matthew. We've talked about this anger thing, haven't we?'

'Right.'

4

'How do you know he was a Turk this time? Did you discuss it with him?'

'Of course we didn't discuss it! We don't sit there having discussions about what are the latest cool fabrics in Istanbul. It's just bloody obvious.'

She looks at me again with that one eyebrow hitched really high. Then she scribbles something in her notes. Or maybe she just quick-sketches a picture of a gun and a clip of bullets. She doesn't fool me. She's lost. I'm lost. All the world is lost.

When they first told me I would have to see a probation officer I was so pissed off. But when I saw Sarah I changed my mind. Even though I think she must be thirty-two or thirty-three I think she's incredibly hot. I mean, I know it's ridiculous. How can someone so old still be a babe? But she is. At sixteen I might be pushing it, but I've heard that some women go for younger guys.

She has wrinkles around her eyes but that doesn't stop me wanting to have sex with her every time I see her. During most of our sessions, I have to sit nursing one. I have a horrible feeling she knows. Though I've never noticed her gaze passing across my groin, I think most women who knew you had a stiffy wouldn't be able to resist sneaking a look, because most women are only human. I'm not saying I look like Leonardo DiCaprio. I'm just saying that I figure a lot of the women out there have as many dirty thoughts as men do. Or as I do.

Factoid number three: girls have dirty thoughts too. Deal with it.

And she smells great. I'd like to ask her what perfume she wears. Maybe I could buy her some.

'Sometimes,' says Sarah, 'I suspect you are making it all up.'

'That's right. I make it all up.'

'I didn't say I *believe* it. I said I suspect it.'

'Same difference.'

'No, it isn't. Think about it.' And she crosses her legs, and her black nylons hiss and that just about makes me pop, but not quite.

I bite my knuckle.

She closes the file and pushes her chair about a quarter of a centimetre back from the table. This is how she signals Time's Up. 'You seem so distracted, Matt. I wish you'd tell me what's going on in that head of yours.'

Is she winding me up? If she can cross her legs like that and not know what's going on in the head of a sixteen-year-old boy, then I don't think she's much of a probation officer.

'Next time I'm going to try something new. Are you prepared to work with me?'

Something new? Word association? Truth drugs? Bashing feather pillows until you cry? Sometimes Sarah seems to think she's a shrink. Duh. I want to say, Hey, you're just here to report my attendance and to tick boxes. Instead I shrug a cautious 'yes'.

Sarah gets up and holds open the door. I stay in my chair for a few extra, unnecessary moments, just to irritate her. When I do get up to leave I try to make eye contact with her but she's already waving in her next freak show, a girl my own age. This girl is a mess. In particular, her hair is a disaster. Judging by the cuts on her scalp, she looks like she tried to trim her own hair with long-handled tree-pruning shears.

As the two of us pass in the doorway I don't look at her and she doesn't look at me, and I'm glad, because if you ask me, she looks like a *real* train-wreck. Whooooooo!

And I'm out of there, and that's me fried for the week.

2

Don't Make Me Sit Next to Her

On my way to school the next day, instead of taking the bus I walk. This makes me late, which is of course deliberate. It's not far, and anyway I do *the count* better on foot.

It was Jake who taught me the count.

I wait for a stream of traffic to come by and the count goes like this: Peugeot 206, twenty-nine seconds; Ford Ka, forty-three seconds; Toyota Corolla, sixty-three seconds. This is all without breaking any glass and without special equipment, you understand. Jake was king, of course, and he could beat me on any of these, but my own speeds are pretty good.

Then a Vauxhall Corsa comes by and that has me scratching my head. Every lock has its quirks and the Corsa is a ticklish one. Jake got into one once but it took him well over three minutes, whereas I've never got into one. I had a go but someone came along before the lock sprung and we had to run for it. Anyway, the game is to count off your personal best for each motor and to see if you can get it to run *in sequence*: your fastest time, followed by your next fastest and so on. You only ever get so far and then something stupid like one of those butt-ugly road-licking kit cars comes along and you have to start again.

If the count ever lines up, one after the other all in the proper order, I wonder what will happen. Maybe something really great. Maybe something terrible. Maybe the end of the world.

Jake taught me all I know about getting into cars. He was the twoc-meister, the undisputed crown prince when it came to taking motors. He had the hot fingers. My dad said he had a touch like a midwife. That's creepy talk. It's when my dad is trying to be funny, but he's not. Though it's true that Jake had the touch.

Most of the time we didn't even take the cars. They were like sardine cans waiting to be rolled back, and we just liked opening them up. The car manufacturers might just as well have put giant sardine-can keys on the tops of the cars.

Jake came up with this cool idea where we ran off some business cards on the computer. The cards read: *Your car was checked today by the NEIGHBOURHOOD WATCH SCHEME. It took only (blank) seconds to enter your car and poke around in the glove compartment, where we found (blank –* we would write things like 'condom', 'g-string', etc. in this space*). Please take greater care in future and have a nice day.* With the blanks neatly filled in, we would leave the card on the seat for the driver to find.

We even did a police car once. You're dying to ask, aren't you? Thirty-nine seconds.

I arrive at school late, so I have to log in with the school secretary. I lie and show her my hands and tell her I've been to see the quack. She looks sympathetic and produces the book. I sign in late and then go straight through.

I enter the classroom quietly. It's heads-down time. GCSEs approaching. Crap! Actually, I don't mind English. It's probably the only exam I will pass. I don't care about the rest. History? Who gives a stuff? Maths? The Black Arts. Religious Ed.? Every lesson makes me lose the will to live.

'How good of you to join us, Mister Norris.' It's Butt, head-of-year, playing with the big gold ring on his finger and chipping in with his customary low-level sarcasm. He's all right is Butt. Could chill out a bit, though. 'At the hospital again, were we? Case of sleeping sickness, was it? Never mind, sit down and let's crack on.'

Butt always comes this 'we' thing. 'Done our homework, have we?' 'Forgotten where we parked our brains, have we?' I say nothing and look round for a chair, and to my horror there is only one free, and it's next to her. Debbie Summerhill.

Butt is already laying out the work on the desk next to Debbie. I hesitate. Butt spots it. 'No, Debbie won't bite you: she's a vegetarian.'

Titters around the room. Some of the other girls look up. Butt prepares another cheap shot but he sees my cheeks flaming – I hate it when that happens – so he backs off. Like I say, he's mostly all right. Debbie has her head down. She squints at me sideways and then continues with her work. I settle into the seat and she shifts away, maybe a quarter of an inch.

I'm not afraid of her. It's just that I've never spoken a single word to her.

Plus, I don't think you should be made to sit next to someone after you've spent practically the whole night thinking about her nude. It's embarrassing. I mean, what if she was somehow able to guess? What if she is a mind reader? You do get people who can see into your mind. I turn the pages of the textbook, trying not to think about her short skirt under the desk.

I'm still leafing through the pages when Debbie says, 'It's page twelve.'

'I know that,' I say, and it comes out too quick and too sharp, in a voice that's a kind of quack. I've no idea why.

Debbie blinks at me, shrugs and gets on with her work. And I know I'm a dickhead. A dickhead who sounds like a duck. I hate myself.

Towards the end of the lesson Butt sneaks up behind me. I try to shield my work from him but he touches my shoulder so I have to sit back and let him give it the once over.

'That all you've managed?' he says.

I flex my fingers to show how the pen is cramping my hands, but he doesn't go away. He hunkers down beside me.

'Matthew, you can't use that as an excuse for ever.' His voice is very low, almost a whisper, but I know that

Debbie and some of the other kids in the class are straining to listen. 'In fact, if you practise with the pen, then within a couple of weeks you won't know the difference – and look! Look at me, Matthew! Hey, I asked you to look at me, please!'

He's got this annoying thing where he insists that you look him in the eye when he's having a go at you. It's not natural.

'That's better. Now, I'm saying you used to write loads of really good stuff for me and I want you to – look at me, Matthew! Don't do that while I'm talking!'

'I am looking at you!'

'You are now, but you keep drifting off and this is important. It might be the most important thing I ever say to you.'

'I'm listening. And looking. I am.'

He breathes in and fixes his gaze on me. Totally unnatural, all this eye contact stuff. Totally unnatural and unnecessary. Then finally he breathes out and says, 'You've got a choice. Either you let this thing beat you or you get back to your schoolwork. You're a clever lad and I don't want to see you blow it all away with more stupidity. Do you understand?'

I don't really know what his big point is – I mean, behind the obvious one – but I nod as if I do.

'Good. Now, why were you late this morning?'

Later, when the bell goes at the end of the lesson Debbie catches me watching her pack her stuff away. She has this pencil case decorated with felt-tip drawings of hearts and flowers and other girlie-guff, but everything about her is so delicate and precise as she tucks away her pens and stacks her books.

She looks up. 'What?' She employs a perfect, clean, pink little-finger to park a lock of hair behind her ear. It makes me shiver.

'Nothin',' I say.

She draws herself to her full height and gives me a look as if to say she *knows* I'm really a werewolf out of school.

How can I answer her properly? How can I say: 'Debbie, I want to come round your house when your mum and dad are out one evening, and I want to sit on your sofa and watch a video and hold your hand all night and snog you until my mouth is sore.' Honestly, I'd be satisfied with just that. Well, not satisfied. But that would do it for me right now. That would be enough.

The rest of the day passes in a blur. Because of Jake appearing at my window all the time, I'm not sleeping too well, and I can't concentrate, either. When the final bell goes I try to recall one single thing I learned in school today. Nothing comes to mind. A whole day's education. Maths, down the tube; History, up in smoke; even English, out of the window.

I walk home with Druce and put the same question to him. 'Eh?' he says.

Now, Druce is not the sharpest knife in the kitchen drawer, but he's a decent sort. 'Come on, Druce. Tell me one thing you learned today.'

'Eh?'

I give up. See, the thing about Druce is he doesn't even seem to know that he's supposed to learn things at school. I'll forgive anyone for being so dense that none of it sticks. But you should at least have some understanding of how much is *not* going in. 'You're thick, Druce. Thick as a brick.'

'That's me: thick,' he says, as if it's something to be proud of. Then he shows me this broad smile that reveals a big gap in his teeth.

Right then, something strange happens. I don't see her until she's right in my face. It's the spooky girl, the train-wreck, the one I saw in Sarah's office. The one with the haircut from doom. She appears as if from nowhere.

She's wearing one of those army-surplus combat jackets and her eyes are painted with mascara and black eyeliner and she's clicking her fingers and humming a tune as she walks down the street. Before I know it, she's got her face right in mine, so close I can smell the sweet, sugary gum she's chewing. And she clicks her fingers again and sways slightly and sings right in my face, a tune I think I recognise:

Na na na na na na na na
Na na na na na na na na

Then she's gone.

I look at Druce and he's looking at me with wide-open eyes and a gormless, amused expression on his face. He has his hands stuffed deep in his trouser pockets and he leans forward, wrinkling his nose, as if sniffing

at something. 'Hey, were that your girlfriend then?'
I try to slap his ear but he's too quick for me, and he
dances away, laughing, giving me grief.
'Druce, Druce, you'll die for that.'

3

You Want Fries with That?

Get home. Dad at kitchen table, drinking tea, reading a newspaper. He raises his eyebrows at me. I raise mine back. He jiggles his eyebrows at me. I put quick end to silly eyebrows game and go upstairs.

'Hey! Get back here!' he roars.

I come back down. He jabs a finger at the rucksack I've just dropped on the floor at the foot of the stairs. I look at him and he raises his eyebrows at me again, so I pick up the bag and hang it – with theatrical delicacy – on one of the hooks under the stairs. He goes back to reading his newspaper and I slink up to my room.

Someone's been in. They never bother tidying it, so that means they've just been in to snoop. That's okay. Snoop away. The thing you're looking for is in my head anyway, and even I don't know where I left it.

It will be an hour before Mum gets back to make supper, so I've got plenty of time to email Jools. I text Jools twice daily and I email her once a day. I've done that ever since the afternoon of Jake's funeral, to which she didn't come. I haven't missed a single day.

16

I email her with information about my day, about some of the thoughts I have. I even tell her about the doom-haircut girl. Then I take the plunge and tell her about sitting next to Debbie Summerhill.

I mean, I don't tell her *everything*. You don't tell girls everything about what's going on in a bloke's head. If they ever guessed they'd never speak to you again. There seems to be an unwritten agreement among guys that you can tell girls maybe about 10 per cent. Not even that. Five per cent. Less. I don't know what they'd do if they knew the half of it. Probably take themselves off to another planet with a rocket ship full of frozen embryos. Nah. They couldn't build a decent rocket, and they know it. But anyway, I leave out all the hot thoughts I've had about Debbie and just tell Jools that I fancy her. Debbie, that is, not Jools. I used to fancy Jools, even though she was my brother's girlfriend – yet another thing to keep quiet about. I don't know if I'd still fancy her. I've heard about the scars, though I haven't had a chance to see them for myself. I think I would probably still fancy her whether she was scarred or not. Because it's the person you go after, isn't it? Not what they look like. Well, it is when you get to know them in the way I got to know Jools.

What I'd like from Jools is for her to advise me. Tell me what to do to get to know Debbie. How not to blow it. She's a year older than me and she's been through a lot more. If she would just email me with a little wise counselling, that would be great.

But she never answers my emails or my text messages. Never.

I think it was bad that she didn't come to Jake's funeral. I mean, the weather was rotten, but that's no excuse. I think her folks should have been there, too. After all, Jake was always round their place. He used to fix stuff for them, fix her dad's car, all that. But they didn't show up. My guess is that they refused to let Jools come along, too. They no doubt blamed Jake, or maybe me and Jake, for what happened to Jools' face.

My first text messages used to say *pls call me. Mat.* Then *why wont u call me?* Then, after some weeks, I started sending weird texts to get her attention. I really blew it with *Jake has message 4 U.* I know that's freaky, even cruel, but I was so upset with her for not replying. Anyway, I still send her two texts per day, lately with little lines from poems or songs. Nothing works.

I get called down for supper. Yellow haddock. Incredibly yellow haddock. I wonder what they put on it to make it so yellow. Or maybe it's all the toxic waste they pour into the sea turning the fish luminous. I have to be careful what I say about the food Mum prepares for me. She's kind of sensitive.

Supper is always a heavy session. Before the accident, Jake and I would just grab something and go to our rooms or watch TV. Now, we have to sit down at the same time and make conversation. It's agony. It's called 'Being A Family Again'. The pattern is two forkfuls of whatever nuclear waste is on the plate and then Dad asks me to tell him about my day at school. But tonight he's distracted. Mum has her head down, too.

I put down my knife and fork. 'Have I done something?' I say.

'What?' says Dad. 'No, son. It's me, I was miles away.'

I look at Mum. She says, 'Your dad had some difficult news today.'

'What news?'

'Oh, they're laying people off at work. I might lose my job.'

Dad has worked as a fitter at Jig and Brace for twenty-two years. He'd got Jake a good job at Jig and Brace. Mum and Dad were so proud of Jake when, on his first morning, he and Dad went off to work together. Everything Jake did made them proud.

'They can't do that!' I yell.

'They can, son. They do it all the time.'

'We're not standing for that!' I hear myself shouting, too loud. 'You've been loyal to those bastards! They make huge profits! We're not taking this lying down.'

I didn't realise it at first but I'm already on my feet, ready for a punch-up with the fat-cat money-grabbing suits on the board of directors at Jig and Brace. My eyes are wet. I feel like I'm going to cry and I don't know why.

Dad smiles. 'Sit down, Matt. Come on, sit down. It's good that you want to fight for things, but I've got to tell you I don't like the job. Never have.'

'What?' I sit down, pick up my fork and push my yellow fish around on the plate. 'Why do you work there, then?'

'Ha! Same reason anyone does. For your mum and you and –'

And, oh shite, he's about to say Jake and we all know it. Dad looks down at his plate as if someone put something surprising and foreign there, and Mum grabs her throat and looks away and then gets up and starts flapping about in the kitchen.

'Eat up, son,' says Dad. 'Tell me about your day. Cheer me up.'

Upstairs, later, I check my email just in case Jools has replied. She hasn't. Nothing but spam. Pollution. Cyber-sewage.

I slip a Slay Dog Dog CD into the slot. I crank the volume right up just to get my old man's heartbeat going and to get him to the bottom of the staircase, then turn it down again before he sets foot on the first step. Fine art.

I plug in my guitar and try to slap out a few heavy chords along with Slay Dog Dog, but I'm crap. My melted fingers can't stretch across the fretboard any more. Actually, that's a joke. I was crap before because I couldn't be bothered to practise. I unplug the guitar and fire up *Gravity Drop!* on the PlayStation.

But I can't get into that, either. Maybe I'm getting bored with it. After ten minutes I'm out of *Gravity Drop!* I don't know what I want. I feel restless. My head feels heavy. I look at my guitar, I look at my PlayStation. Then I take off my shirt and lie down on the bed.

I lie back, listening to the music. My hand drifts to the waistband of my trousers as I think about Debbie Summerhill. It's easy when I'm with Debbie like this.

She lets me undo her buttons. She lets me touch the waistband of her jeans. But here's where something annoying happens. Just when I've got Debbie right where I want her, just when she's smiling and half-naked and leaning forward to kiss me, she changes. And who does she change into?

Doom-crop. Hedgerow-locks. Horror-thatch. Yeh, her. That loser from the probation office.

And I'm thinking: This is my imagination, I'm in control, I'm in charge of this movie. So why does *she* keep showing up? And who the hell is she anyway? I go back and think through the sequence with Debbie again. I take this off, she takes that off and all is fine, but then it happens again. As soon as Debbie is half-naked, the haircut from hell pops up going, '*Na na na na na na.*' And I shout, 'Go away!' Actually, I'm not sure if I shout it or just think it.

Excuse me, I'm trying to have a sexual fantasy here. Why does this horror-movie psycho-bimbo from hell keep forcing her way into my imagination? And why can't I stop it? I'm still feeling furious about this when there's a light tapping on the window. I'm so annoyed about this girl sticking her fright-wig into my sexy dreams that I forget I'm not supposed to look, and then it's too late. Jake has got me.

I even snigger when I see him. It shouldn't be funny, but it is. Like, what are you wearing this time, Jake? Then the sniggers stop as the sick feeling rolls over me, flips my stomach and everything goes into slow motion for three or four seconds before I come out the other side.

I always feel sick when I see Jake. And there is always this noise, like a deep groan but from far away. The groan is one bad note that doesn't fade all the time Jake is there.

He's wearing one of those drudge uniforms you have to put on when you work in a ratburger joint. It's blue and red and he has a baseball cap with the peak tugged low over his eyes. Jake used to have a Saturday job scooping ratburgers and fries when he was saving up for his first car. What a worker he was! He used to come home reeking of diseased fat. He's hovering outside the window, tapping lightly on the glass. He looks cold.

I go over to the window. 'I'm not going to let you in, Jake.'

He mouths something through the glass. It's muffled, so I put my ear to the glass and hear him say something like, 'Why are you looking so thin these days?'

I don't know what he means, but I look up and see myself reflected in the full-length mirror mounted on my wardrobe, and he's right, I'm skin and bone. What's more, my ribcage is luminous yellow under my skin, and it's pulsating gently. I look down at myself and it seems normal, but when I look back in the mirror the ladder of my ribcage is luminous again. I think it must be the toxic waste in the fish I ate earlier.

I look back at Jake and he's holding out a bag, just like in the burger bar; you know, like 'Do you want fries with that?' Maybe Jake is trying to feed me. I relent and open the window and he hands me the bag.

'Eat up, brother of mine, you're a growing boy,' says Jake.

'Thanks,' I say.

'Got to look after my bro.'

But I don't know about this bag. It has a bad weight. I open the bag, reach in and pull out some of its contents. In my hand is a human ear, slightly ragged and bloody at its edge. And a toe. And a finger amputated at the second knuckle. I look deeper into the bag and there are things in it I don't even want to mention.

I glance up from the bag and there is Jake outside the window laughing his head off, and in my hand are these body parts and I start screaming, loud, louder. I start screaming and I don't stop even though no one downstairs can hear me because Slay Dog Dog are laying down some really heavy chords and screaming vocals themselves. But then the track reaches its end and I'm still screaming when my dad bursts into the room. He throws himself at me, and hugs me.

'It's all right son, it's all right,' he says, taking a bag of biscuits out of my hand.

He says this over and over and over and I feel my screaming go away, and then I'm burbling and weeping in my old man's arms like I'm five years old. I'm ashamed of crying like this, but I can't stop myself.

'Easy, easy, son,' my dad goes again. 'It's all right.'

4

Handbags and Glad-rags

So here's what I remember about what happened that night. It's Jools' seventeenth birthday and Jake has a surprise for her. He's got boss tickets for them both to go and see the Lockhearts, who are shite, as everyone knows, but Jools likes them and Jake will even sit through an oozing hour and a half of boy band for her. Yeh, boys with nail-varnish and hair highlights, an evening so greasy it's like diving into a swimming pool filled with chip-oil. That's how far he'd go for her. Or would do if his pal Merrick had turned up with the tickets. Merrick, whose job it was to get four tickets so he and his girlfriend Laura, whom I'd never met, could go along too.

Merrick, you're a TWAT! You hear that, Merrick? If you'd done what you promised, if you'd got those tickets, none of this would have happened and Jake would still be here! Alive! Right now!

I wasn't going to the concert. First, I wasn't invited. But I wouldn't watch the Lockhearts if they were crooning on the balcony of our flat. Not even if they were giving out free beer. Not even if they had naked Page 3 girls trying to drag you on to our balcony to watch them because the Lockhearts are not even worth talking about.

But I was home that evening when Jools arrived. The plan was for Merrick and his girl to collect Jake and Jools from our house and go on to the concert. Jake was upstairs, patting his face with knock-off Givenchy aftershave, and sticking bits of tissue on a shaving cut, so I answered the door.

I nearly fell over. I'd never seen anything more beautiful than Jools that night, I swear. She stood in the doorway, smiling shyly, her dark eyes opened wide at me, as if she wanted me to approve. Her silky black hair framed her pale face and her lips were the colour of dark cherries. She wore a long, black leather coat all the way down to her heels, and the coat hung open at the front to reveal the tiniest skirt and sensational legs.

'Aren't you going to let me in?'

I was speechless. My tongue stuck to the roof of my mouth. I must have swallowed before mumbling something stupid. She squeezed past me and I could smell the shampoo on her hair.

'I'm late,' she said. 'Are Merrick and Laura here yet?'

'No,' was all I could manage to say.

'Where's Jake? Are you all right, Matt? You look like you've seen a ghost.'

Mum came to the rescue, bustling in from the kitchen. 'Ooh, ooh, ooh,' she said, as if her rheumatic pains were playing her up. 'You look lovely, my flower.

25

Lovely. Matt, go and tell Jake that this vision of loveliness has arrived.'

'I'm not saying that.'

'Just go and tell him!' Mum took Jools through to the lounge. 'Come and sit down, my flower.'

I trudged upstairs. Jake was still in the bathroom, hitting the Givenchy. 'You smell like a tart's handbag,' I said.

'Shall I chin you?'

'No.'

'Is Merrick here yet?' said Jake.

'No. But Jools is.'

Jake peeled the bits of tissue off his face and made a pig-snort in the mirror – I don't know why. Then, as he shuffled past me to go downstairs, he patted my cheek.

'You could at least have got me a ticket, you bastard!' I shouted after him.

'Them tickets are rare as rocking 'orse shit,' he said, clattering down the stairs. 'Anyway, you don't even like the Lockhearts.'

No, I thought, but if I got to sit next to Jools, it would be worth it. Hell, I'd volunteer to be Ozzy Osbourne's toilet attendant if it somehow got me a seat next to Jools. How is it my brother gets to sit next to her, while I rot at home?

Merrick was cutting it close. Where could he have got to? I sat in the room with Jake and Jools, while Mum and Dad made all these unhelpful comments. 'Perhaps you should give Merrick another call?'

But Jake had already rung his number twice. He'd spoken to Merrick's mum, who had no idea where

26

Merrick was, and didn't know anything about any tickets.

'Shall I run you down in the car?' Dad had asked. 'What's the good of that without any tickets,' Mum had said. 'They might have left them at the box office,' he said. 'That's a thought,' she said. 'I'll phone the box office.'

Nope.

The concert started at 8 p.m. At 8.30 we were still all sitting in the lounge.

'And here's the pair of you all done up in your glad-rags,' said Dad.

Jake looked at my old man. It was that special look, the one that says: Thanks, Dad, thanks a bunch.

Dad took out his wallet. 'Here. Go up to that new restaurant on the High Street. Make a night of it.'

'I've already eaten,' said Jools.

'Go up to that fancy wine bar then. What's it called? Pillocks?'

'Picklocks,' said Jake.

'Well. Buy a bottle of champagne. Not your birthday every day, is it, princess?'

Jools and Jake hauled themselves out of their chairs. Then Jools looked at me. 'Want to come with us, Matt? We might need cheering up.'

'What?' I said.

'That's all right isn't it, Jake?' She knew Jake could be heavy weather when he was down.

Jake surveyed me glumly. 'Yeh,' he said, pocketing Dad's banknotes. 'Yeh.'

We walked together up to Picklocks wine bar on the High Street. Picklocks is one of those super-trendy glass-and-chrome joints with fat, squashy leather seats. I didn't think I'd get away with it. As soon as we walked through the door I knew it wouldn't work. I might as well have had *Underage* tattooed on my forehead. Jake and Jools were okay, but I wasn't even dressed right for that kind of place. I tell you, even the barman waxed his hair and wore smart black chinos, a black designer belt and a black turtleneck shirt. Ha ha ha ha ha ha ha ha!

The barman took one look at me and said, 'Aroldizee, then?' He shook his head. 'Yintoldenuff.'

'Coke for the lad,' said Jake, all suave, as if he were a hundred years old himself. 'And champagne and two glasses for us.'

The barman sniffed, filled a glass with ice and sprayed it with Coke from a gun, all as if he thought he was James Bond. He set the glass down in front of me and went off in search of Jake's champagne. Jools and I found a squashy seat by the window. 'I'll let you have a sip of mine,' she said.

'You'd better.'

Jake brought the champagne to us in a silver bucket. I didn't think that was right. That snotty barman should have carried it over. If you're paying for champagne, you might as well make the monkey jump. But I didn't say anything. Jake was in charge.

We sat and drank the champagne, or rather Jake and Jools let me gulp from their glasses when the barman wasn't watching. But the mood was depressed. The ticket fiasco hung over Jake like a black cloud. Jools did her best to make light of it, saying it didn't matter, but I knew how hard Jake had worked to spring those tickets. Overtime at the ratburger hut, pulling in the top seats, all that.

He was gazing into the bottom of the empty champagne bottle when we all heard a slow purring, a deliciously faint chugging from across the road. Our heads all turned at once to look through the window. Directly opposite was an expensive restaurant called Kefi, the sort of place celebrities might hang out, if we had any celebrities in Wickhamstead, which we don't.

'Yes!' said Jake. 'Yes! Yes! Yes!'

It was a silver-grey Ferrari Testarossa, parking up outside the restaurant. The driver hauled himself out, a little baldy guy with a grand-and-a-half tailored suit that couldn't hide a huge spilling gut. Out of the passenger seat climbed a suntanned bottle-blonde. The woman fell over on her ridiculously high heels as she stepped on to the kerb. Together they examined the pavement as if a little hand had come out of the gutter and grabbed her ankle. Then they went inside the restaurant.

'Oh no!' went Jools, covering her face with her hands.

'How long to be safe?' Jake said to me. Not that he didn't know himself: it was a master-and-apprentice routine, like he was still teaching me.

'With a gut like that he's going to have starter, main course, dessert, coffee, brandy, cigar *and* a fart in the bog upstairs.'

'Well, let's not be greedy,' said Jake. 'Let's just do the ninety minutes.'

'Plus stoppage time,' I suggested.

'You're not going to, are you?' said Jools.

'I promised to make your birthday memorable,' said Jake, rising from his seat. 'And memorable it shall be!'

5

Get ahead with a Mohawk

'Your dad tells me you had another episode.'

Episode. This is Sarah's word for the gale-force-nine freak-storm where I rip my throat out by the act of screaming and my eyeballs melt and I'm turned into a quivering jelly by the sight of a packet of chocolate-chip cookies. An episode. Like it was just a half-hour of Australian soap opera after school.

'Yeh. I had one. An episode.'

'Jake came to see you again? At the window?'

'Kind of.'

'Are you going to continue to act all cool? Or are you going to tell me about it?'

I'm a little disappointed with Sarah today. Maybe it's the warmer spring weather, but she's not wearing those gorgeous black tights that hiss like a nest of snakes every time she crosses her legs. In fact, her legs are bare and I can see that they are, well, hairy. Not *that* hairy. But hairy enough. I'm not saying that she's like one of those women who run Girl Guide troops or who advocate natural childbirth or whatever. I mean, it's not as if she's *furry*. It's just that the sun is streaming through the window, past a little spring collection of daffodils and irises on the window sill, and is illuminating this very fine, dark, treacle-coloured down she has on the ridge of her shin. It's not sexy at all, but I can't seem to avert my gaze from her legs. I don't want to look at them, but I can't take my eyes off those bristling hairs.

'Hello, Matt,' she goes. 'Anyone at home?'

'I'm thinking,' I say.

'Don't think about it. Talk about it.'

'That's just it. When I try to talk about it, I go blank.' This is true. Whenever I think about it, it's like I'm wasted. Like when you smoke some of what Jake used to call skunk. It's a crap smoke that spoils all the fun because it's too stupidly strong and all you can do is hang your mouth open and dribble. I hate that shit. Well, that's what happens to me when I think about what happened that night. I just get wasted.

I try to explain this to Sarah. I ask her if she's ever smoked any skunk, so she will know what I mean.

'If I ever had,' she says, arching a single eyebrow, 'then I'm hardly likely to admit it to you, am I?'

'Why not?' I try to sound indignant.

'Because, for one thing, it's illegal; and for another thing, you would rush straight out of this door and tell all your friends.'

'So you have?'

'As a matter of fact, no, I haven't. But I'm not the subject here. You are, Matt.'

'So I'm supposed to tell you everything and you tell me nothing, is that it?'

But she's not falling for it. 'Yes, exactly that!' You're the one referred here by the courts, remember! You're the one with the criminal conviction, not me. You stole a car and smashed it up and people were injured. That's why you're here. Isn't that ever going to sink in?'

I offer up a sigh, all theatre. 'Why are you getting at me?'

'No one is getting at you!'

'Oh no? So why are you trying to get inside my head? So why are the courts going to all this trouble? Why not just lock me up?'

Sarah shakes her head slightly. She clasps her hands together under her chin and blinks at me. 'Matt, it must have occurred to you that you could easily have been sent to a youth custody centre. A juvenile prison. And you still can be if you don't co-operate. Have you ever stopped to think that people might be trying to help you?'

'It just doesn't seem fair. I'm supposed to spill the beans about myself and I don't know anything about you. How can I trust you?'

'Oh, heavens! Right: let's make a deal then. You ask your questions and I'll ask mine. We both promise to answer truthfully.'

I instantly suspect a trap. I wish I hadn't started this, because she's outfoxed me.

'Well?' she says.

'All right, but I get to ask first.' I think I can stop this

33

game early enough. She shrugs, so I say, 'Have you got a boyfriend?'

'Yes. His name is Alex. We've been together for five years.'

'Do you have sex with Alex?'

Sarah doesn't blink. 'Of course we do. Not as often as we used to when we first met. But still often. Very good sex, thank you.'

I nod sagely, as if processing this important information. Then I don't know why I ask her this. I don't even want an answer. I don't care. But it just comes out. 'Do you shave your legs?'

'What? What a strange question! Yes, I do on occasion. But I don't lie awake at night worrying about whether my legs need shaving.'

I've obviously puzzled her with that last question. Thing is, I've puzzled myself, too. I mean, what sort of an idiot would ask a question like that? Now I've managed to disgust myself. Anyway, Sarah says it's her turn to ask questions. She asks if I'm ready to answer, and I say yes.

'So what was in the bag, Matt?'

'The bag?'

'Yes. When your dad came upstairs and found you screaming.'

'Nothing. Cookies. Chocolate-chip cookies. That's all that was in the bag. Ridiculous, isn't it? I mean, I was shouting the house down and there was nothing in the bag except these biscuits. Ha.'

'Let me rephrase my question: what did you *think* was in the bag?'

I look out of the window. I look at Sarah's slightly hairy legs. I look anywhere but directly at Sarah's face. I feel my hand flutter to my brow and wipe away a patch of sweat that is forming there. I try to think about the bag. I remember Jake at the window. But everything goes into the awful slo-mo again as the picture in my mind sags and melts. I hear that awful groaning sound, like metal buckling. Coin-sized blisters of sweat form on my brow and I feel my hand flutter up there again.

'Matt?' It's Sarah's voice, calling me out of it. 'Matt!'

I want to speak. I have to tell her. I know I should tell her. I've even shaped my mouth to speak, but nothing is coming out. Finally I'm about to tell her about the horrible bits of maimed bodies that I saw in the bag when the telephone rings.

Saved by the bell.

Sarah snatches up the phone. She never likes to be interrupted during these sessions, so it must be important. I watch her face as she receives some news. She grits her teeth. Then she shivers and touches the back of her neck with her free hand. 'Heck! Oh boy! I'd better come down there right away.'

She's out of her chair. 'I'm sorry about this, Matt,' she says cradling the receiver. 'Really sorry, but I've got to race into town.'

I try to look dismayed but can't conceal my relief. It makes no difference. She's not interested in me any more. She's throwing on her coat, gathering up her handbag, rifling through her cabinet for a file. 'Wait in the reception room until I get back.'

'Can't I just go early?' But I already know the answer. Sarah does everything by the book, and if I leave early, I'll just have to report another day.

'You're still under supervision. So wait.'

'What's happened?' I ask, following her out of the room.

'Just wait here until I get back.' She locks the door behind her, waves at Mrs Took the receptionist and is out of the door. She's flying. She's gone.

Mrs Took takes off her glasses and points with them at a seat. Only now do I realise someone else is sitting in the reception room.

It's her. Scythe-top. Blade-head. Terror-locks.

She's chewing gum and looking dead ahead, but I know she's clocked me. There are three moulded plastic chairs in a line and she's sitting in the middle one, so I have no choice but to sit next to her. I mean, I could make a big thing of lifting one of the seats and setting it down as far as possible away from her, but it would be too much of a statement. Then I think what the hell, and that's exactly what I do. I shift one of the chairs away from her and I fall into it. She sighs heavily. At least she's not going, 'Na na na na na,' and all that.

I pretend to study the ceiling but really I'm watching her at the edge of my vision. She wears drab green army combats: fatigue jacket and trousers and boots bought from Spotwell's Army Surplus on the corner of Tanner Road. I've been there. It's full of cheap crap. She's dressed like she's getting ready to go to Iraq. No, she looks like she's been there but she frightened the

36

terrorists too much so they sent her back. And that haircut. Looks like an Apache dragged her from the wagon train for a scalp-fest but didn't finish the job. No, it looks like . . . aw hell, who cares what she looks like? She's a freak.

Then she blows a bubble of gum and clacks it, really loud, so that Mrs Took looks up at her with an expression of mild disapproval.

I can't help myself. 'That's very impressive,' I say across the room. 'I thought that was a lost skill. A dying art. I didn't know that people still chewed bubble gum in the twenty-first century. I thought it went out with mods and rockers and combat gear and whistling on the way to work. But I think it's great that people like you are keeping these folk-culture things alive.'

She stops chewing and turns to look me in the eye. She holds my gaze for a long time. It's unnerving but I'm determined not to be the one to break. Though just when I blink she looks down into my groin. You know, right into my lap. Then she snorts, as if she's found something desperately funny there, returns her stare to dead ahead, sits on her hands and resumes her furious chewing.

What a cow!

'I couldn't help noticing your adventurous hair-styling,' I say, very polite. 'My compliments. It's quite an edge-of-seat coiffure. What might be termed a radical trim. But might I offer some advice?'

She stops chewing. Then she turns to look at me again. Tilting her head this time. I don't mean just tilting her head slightly, I mean the full ninety degrees, so that her ear is pressed flat against her shoulder, as if she needs to look at me from a completely different angle. She's quite the full circus act, this girl, I'll tell you.

Then she straightens up. 'Advice?' she says. Her voice is surprisingly deep. 'Haven't you worked out what this place is? It's for people with twisted heads. Why would I want advice from someone with a twisted head? You should get a grip.'

Whooooooooooooooooooo! Aren't we the sharp blade? But I'm not ruffled. 'That's an interesting point of view. However, I'd still like to make a suggestion –'

'Sarah has gone to casualty,' she says, cutting me off. 'I overheard Mrs Took telling her on the phone.' At this, Mrs Took looks over her spectacles at us, and goes, 'tut-tut'. 'One of her other twisty-heads has tried to top himself. Just like you might, any day now.'

'What?'

She fails to answer. Just resumes her gum-chewing and her dead-ahead, five-yard stare.

'So you can tell, can you?' I ask her.

'Yep. Can.'

'You've got X-ray vision, have you?'

'If you like.'

'This is fascinating. So why would I be any more likely to top myself than you?'

'I'm not in the topping business.'

'Oh! Really! We're all very relieved! Sarah will be relieved. The admirable Mrs Took will be relieved. I myself am greatly relieved to hear that. This is a special day for me.'

38

'Like to go *on and on and on* about nothing at all, don't you?'

I ignore that shot. 'My suggestion is that you could still salvage it. The hair, I mean. Mohawk. A nice crest has survived from front to back. If you shaved your head completely at the sides you'd be left with a neat ridge of hair, which you could dye crimson or blue. A stunning Mohawk haircut. Very cool. That would put it right.' I smile pleasantly.

She chews rapidly. Target down.

For the next hour we await Sarah's return in an ear-splitting silence.

6

Dreams within Dreams within Dreams

Egg and chips for tea. Lovely, just what I like, proper home-cooked junk food, sitting down with Mater and Pater. Though just as I get a nice golden chip hooked on the end of my fork with which to stab the sunshine-yellow yolk, Mum goes, 'So what did your probation officer have to say to you?'

How to spoil teatime, eh? How to ruin the bursting of an egg yolk. They practise it. They deliberately wait until the wrong moment. Mothers: they should be strangled at birth.

'Not much. We got any sauce?'

Mum gets up from her chair to get me the sauce. Dad puts a hand on her forearm.

'Sit down,' he says. 'The lad's not helpless. He can get up and get it for himself. He hasn't burned his bloody legs.'

Mum sits down. We carry on eating in silence. Then: 'I thought you wanted the sauce,' says Mum.

'Not bothered,' I say.

'I'll get it,' says Mum.

'Don't you dare,' growls Dad. 'Now then, Matt, let's hear a bit about what that Sarah had to say.'

It's always *that Sarah* with Dad. Okay, I don't blame them for being interested. They think I'm holding back something. But how can I tell them that *that Sarah* has been trying to get me to talk about a thing I can't talk about? Now Mum and Dad want me to talk about not talking about the thing I can't talk about.

So I tell them about Sarah rushing off to deal with that kid who'd taken an overdose of pills. They pumped his stomach and he was okay. So I guess he can try it again next week. No, I don't mean that. I wouldn't wish that on anyone. I wish I hadn't said that, not even as a joke. But anyway, it's a good story to report to Mum and Dad, because it serves to illustrate to them how delicate my own state is. How close to the edge I am. How they'd better not push too hard, or I'll be next with a rubber tube down my gullet.

I sigh deeply after reporting this story, and bite into a chip, all as if the boy in question was one of my best friends. But as I look up I see Dad scowling at me. His face says: Don't push your luck.

'But are you making any progress?' Mum wants to know. 'Is this Sarah helping you any?'

'Look, Mum, she's a probation officer, not a shrink. Her job is to try to make sure I don't reoffend, not to find out what went wrong with my upbringing.'

My mum sniffs. I wish I hadn't said that, too, even as a joke.

I love my mum, but she's thick. She thinks that by

going to the probation office once a week I get my criminality and my delinquency sucked out of me a bit at a time until I'm all better and then I can get a job at Jig and Brace for the rest of my life, like Dad. Or like the job that Dad doesn't have now. I know they want me to be like Jake. They want me to live up to the memory of him, be the fine son he was. They want me to do everything that he did. I think they secretly want me to live the life he won't have.

'We know all that,' says Dad. 'But she's there to help you change your ways.'

I look down at my hands. 'My ways are already changed.'

'Well,' says Dad. 'Well.'

After that I don't feel too good. I mess around with *Gravity Drop!* but I can't stay interested. I strum a few chords on my guitar before slinging it on the bed. I'm too agitated.

I blame it on that girl. Skull-fright. Razor-pelt. What she said has somehow got to me. About how I'm a candidate for topping myself, just like the other one. I'm not. I might play-act and sigh over the egg and chips, but there's no way I would ever do such a thing. I don't know how or why I let her get to me.

I shut down my equipment and climb into bed. Only I've left on the power light on the PlayStation and it stares back at me like a single red eye. I can't be bothered to get my arse out of bed to switch it off, so I close my eyes and try to sleep. I'm not even in the mood to think about Debbie Summerhill nude. Nor Sarah. That hairy-leg thing has spoiled it for me. Anyway, like I say, I blame it all on the freak. Chop-top. Hairbrush-zombie. Her.

It really annoys me when a picture of Chop-top, nude, comes floating into my head. And in this picture she's taken my advice and got herself a Mohawk hair-cut, dyed electric blue. And I have to admit there's something twisted-sexy about her, even though I don't want anything to do with her.

I open my eyes to banish the picture of her, and instead I see the red light from the console. At least, I think it's the red light, but it has moved. It has floated clean across the room. All the way to the window.

I know this can't be right, so I get out of bed and step across to the window myself, towards the source of the red light, which hovers unsteadily on the other side of the glass. Only now I see it isn't a red light at all; it's an eye. Jake's eye. He's got this one red-bulb electronic eye and one ordinary eye, like he's half-robot, a cyborg.

And he's dressed as a girl. He smiles, sadly.

When I say he's dressed as a girl, I mean he's like a bad pantomime-dame figure of a girl. He has a blond wig tied in bunches. He has make-up slapped all over his face – rouge cheeks, turquoise eye-shadow, false batting eyelashes and a thick smear of pink lipstick. And he's wearing a long blue gingham dress with puff-sleeves.

I want to throw up.

But I don't. I've had enough. This time I know I'm going to do something about it all. I've had enough of

43

Jake's games. I wrench open the window and open my mouth and out it comes. Really. It's like emptying both barrels of a shotgun right in his face. Every vile and dirty word I can think of gets packed into a single sound and my mouth opens like a furnace and this blast of air comes boiling out of it like a belch of black oil-burning smoke. It's so strong it blows Jake's wig right off into the night; so fierce it lifts up the hem of his dress and wraps it round his head and blows him right out of there.

He's gone.

I still want to vomit but I also want to slam shut the window and scuttle back under my bedclothes, but I can't because something bad is bothering me.

There's a knock on the door. It's Dad. 'You all right, son?'

'Yeh. I'm all right.'

'Thought I heard a yell.'

'I'm all right, Dad. Thanks.'

'Okay. 'Night, son.'

Finally I do close the window. But I don't want to get back into bed yet. First I have to do what I often do, which is check that I'm not dreaming. This isn't as easy as it sounds. See, when dreaming, you might sometimes dream that things are perfectly normal. I might just have dreamed that Dad knocked on the door and asked me if everything is okay. You can pinch yourself and all that storybook crap, but you might just be dreaming that you are pinching yourself. What is there to say that you are not dreaming? I might be dreaming that I'm

44

telling you all this. You might be dreaming that you're hearing it. Don't think about it. It can drive you mad.

But I heard there *is* this one test, and I do sort of rely on it. That is, if you switch on a light and it comes on, you're probably not dreaming. If you are dreaming, what happens is that the light will come on but with a few seconds' delay; or a completely different light will come on. You could open a fridge door and instead of the fridge light coming on, your reading lamp comes on. Anyway, if that happens, then you know you're dreaming.

I don't know who worked this out. I don't even know if it's true, but I do it anyway. So I switch on my bedside lamp and it comes on as normal. I switch it off again. Then I get back into bed and try to get to sleep.

But I can't, because there's that thing still bothering me about Jake.

When that wind blew up his dress, he wasn't wearing anything underneath. And he had nothing there. Instead of where his poonie should be, there was nothing. Well, not nothing exactly. I don't suppose females think of it as nothing. What I mean is, he was a girl underneath. Like he'd had a sex change. Like he wasn't my brother, but my sister.

Oh, Jake.

I lie back in the dark. I think I might tell Sarah about that. I really think I might.

7

An Idiot's Guide to the
On-screen Hotwire

So let me tell you how it goes. Jake is already across the road, casing the Testarossa, while Jools and I watch from behind the plate glass of the wine bar. I know you want me to say that Jools is whimpering and going, 'No, please, don't spoil the evening, don't get us into trouble,' and all that. But you'd be wrong there.

Jools, you see, loves it. She's had a disappointment, too, don't forget, over the damn tickets. She wants some fun. She wants the vroom, vroom, vroom. Of course she does. Factoid number nine: women are human, too. Deal with it.

And it's beautiful to watch Jake at work. I've studied him, and still I marvel. He's across the road, talking to no one on his phone. He stops near the Testarossa, gesticulating mildly, slightly irritated with the fictional body on the other end of the line, just a guy yakking into his mobile. He's so fast with the Stuart you barely see it. But I see it.

Some people call them a Slim Jim, but that gives it away, of course. If Jake and I were talking in front of

Mum and Dad, we could hardly say, 'Let's go out and, by the way, bring the Slim Jim', or even 'Jim'. Dad may be the wrong side of fifty, but he's been around the corner. He knows what he knows. Hence Stuart. 'Shall we see if Stuart fancies a game of snooker, eh Matt?' Or: 'Stuart wants a game of footie.' And so on.

Jake first taught me how to work with a bent wire coat-hanger. You untwist it, reshape it, tape off the sharp ends and it does the job well. More importantly, if you think you're getting pulled, you can turn it back into a coat-hanger and it looks less like you're going equipped. 'No, Officer, I'm just going home to hang up my coat.'

Yeh, well. So Jake has an aluminium strip instead. And it telescopes, to not much longer than a pen, so neatly you can keep it in your inside pocket. He made it himself on the lathe at Jig and Brace. Put the hooks and curves in according to his own specifications. And Jake is such a good brother he made me one, too, for my birthday. That night I went out and nicked a Jag, and crashed it, too.

Jake is so good he still has his mobile glued to one ear, flicks open his Stuart and digs it under the rubber seal of the driver's window. I'm counting. And before I've got to five seconds he's got the door open. Can you believe the people who make these things? They *want* us to get in. Really, they do.

Jake explained it to me. They could build a car like Fort Knox if they wanted to. But the car companies are hand-in-glove with the component manufacturers. Every time some junkie wants to rip out a CD player to sell for the price of a sandwich, the insurance firms cough up for an overpriced replacement. Good business. It's a scam. Those old boys in their suits raise their champagne glasses to twocers and junkies everywhere, every day. Of course they do.

Five seconds, though! Give respect. Heap praise on the man. Applaud where applause is due. Because Jake is the best of the best.

He waits his moment: street empty; traffic clear. The alarm squeals as Jake opens the door. As expected. Jake is cool under pressure. He ducks under the dash and in less than two seconds he has disabled the alarm. He backs out, nippy, closes the door, and rolls underneath the car. I tell you, this boy is so hot he won't even dirty his jacket.

The next couple of minutes it's just a matter of waiting, to see if anyone heard the first squeal of the alarm. If fatso inside is too busy trying to impress his tanned tart in front of the wine waiter, then he won't have heard a thing. But you have to be careful. Some men are more tuned in to their cars than they are to their girlfriends. Jake told me that with these guys you could get their girlfriend's phone number right from under their noses, but if you so much as glanced at the upholstered interior of their modified motor they'd get twitchy. Jake told me about one guy who spends his Sunday afternoons cleaning his wheel rims with a toothbrush but who wouldn't think of brushing his teeth before getting into bed with his wife. Men and motor cars. Figure it out.

Like a pale moon, a waiter's face appears at the restaurant door, but then he's gone. It's all cool. Jake rolls out from under the car, gets the door open again and dives in. He's under the dash now. Anyone passing in the street and admiring this nice motor won't even see him.

You've seen the next bit a hundred times in the movies. Rip off the plastic from around the steering column. Strip the insulation from a couple of electrical wires. Make contact. Engine sparks into life. Drive away.

Bullshit.

Who writes these movies? I've heard that scriptwriters in Hollywood get paid thousands and thousands of dollars for writing this crap. Are they thick? Haven't they ever been car breakers themselves? Sometimes it's hard to know exactly who to blame for all the stupidity in this world. You do that Hollywood thing and you've got just as much chance of shorting out the engine system as you have of driving away.

Old cars were easier, but these days you have to rip out the panelling from under the dash with pliers, because you have to get power to the dash. You attach a wire to the positive side of the coil wire. Then you get out again and get under the bonnet. Jake hasn't wasted his time under the car, where he would have used his Stuart to flip the release catch. Once you're under the bonnet, you need to attach that wire from the coil to the battery positive. That's power-to-dash sorted. Then you just touch the small starter solenoid wire with the pliers so that it crosses with the positive battery wire, and the engine cranks right up.

Once he's under the bonnet, Jake does all this in maybe four seconds. Then he's back inside the car and he's away. Not counting the time he was lying under the car, he's well under a minute.

'How does he do it?' says Jools, breathless with admiration.

'I can do it too,' I point out as we get up to leave.

'I know you can,' she says, touching my arm.

'Just not so fast,' I admit.

Our job is to check out the restaurant for a minute or two after Jake has gone, just to see if anyone has heard the car being driven off. But fatso is probably too busy slurping his lobster-bisque starter and eyeballing his girlfriend's silicone tits, so we move off up to the riverside, where we've already arranged for Jake to pick us up.

We have to wait a couple more minutes before Jake cruises up to us. 'All aboard,' he shouts as we climb inside.

It's really a kind of two-seater, so Jools has to sit on my lap, but I'm not complaining!

Then we're off. 'The Ferrari Testarossa,' Jake quips in his best BBC star-car English, fiddling with the radio to whip up some sounds. 'Mid-engine sports coupé. Steel frame with aluminium and fibreglass panels. Manual transmission. Independent front and back suspension. Maximum speed approximately one hundred and eighty miles per hour. Zero to sixty in five seconds. It's a piece of shit.'

'Really?' I say, admiring the electrically adjustable seats and the hand-stitched hide trim of the interior. 'Looks all right to me.'

'Me too,' says Jools.

'Naw. It has grunt, I'll give you that. But it's a fat arse for fat arses. Handles like a tank. Overweight and over-rated. Ugly 1980s piece of show. Thank God we didn't pay the hundred grand for it.'

And that makes the three of us laugh like hyenas. Jake turns on to a country road, taking us out of town, and he boots the accelerator.

Vroom, vroom.

So we do the Testarossa hot-sauce up to the old Roman road, which is, as everybody knows, straight as a string. Jake stops the car, lets the engine purr for a mo, then hammers the accelerator and we count up the zero to sixty, and after that the hundred, which I call at thirteen seconds. Jake slows, we turn around and do it again in the other direction.

I see what CDs we have. As expected, it's the Jeremy Perm motoring show, the BBC's idea of driving music: Dire Straits, the Allman Brothers, the Eagles. All barely music at all. The sort of stuff your grandma might shuffle round the dance floor to at a wedding reception. 'Drive-time', as highly recommended by Jeremy Perm. Music to do the washing-up to, more like.

Jake puts the overstuffed tank through its paces. With the road completely clear, he does a couple of handbrake turns. I ask him if I can have a go, so we swap places and Jake gets Jools back to himself. They instantly start snogging as I rev up for my turn, and already he's got his tongue so far down her throat he's gonna taste what she had for her tea.

My handbrake turns are cool enough. That means good. Double-plus-good. Here we go. Stay in second gear, beef up to about twenty-five, left paw on the handbrake button. Then whip the steering wheel sharply to the right. The trick lies in not dragging on the handbrake too early. You have to wait until you're rocked to the side, then you slam it on, and keep your thumb on the button. If you're good, you can spin 180 degrees. And you crap yourself.

Damn, I'm good, but Jake and Jools snog right through my turns and they don't even notice. I get fed up of this so I set off up the Roman road again to find a bit of speed. Jake unglues himself from Jools' mouth for long enough to complain about the crappy music. I suggest he looks for something better.

'Well, well, well!' says Jake, finding a plastic bag in the glove compartment. 'What do we have here?'

It's a bag of fine-chopped green leaves. 'Hedge clippings,' says Jake, opening the bag and sticking his nose right inside. 'Yo-yo grass. Whacky-baccy.'

'Isn't that illegal?' says Jools. 'Perhaps we should call the police.'

That gets a laugh.

8

A Skull-boy's Life

School. I've taken to winding up everyone by calling it 'skull'. As in 'Hurry up, you'll be late for skull!' Or: 'What did you do in skull today, sonny?'

It just gets that flicker of a response. A little double-take. Especially from teachers. They flicker another glance at you to see if you're taking the piss, then they assume that they misheard. Not Dad, though. He knows what I'm up to. I cross the line when at breakfast I say, 'Has anyone seen my skull-books?'

'I'll rap my knuckles on your skull if you don't cut it out.'

'What?' I cry, all innocence, all put upon and picked on.

'You heard!' goes Dad.

I give Mum that wide-eyed, open-mouthed thing, but she just frowns at me.

The teachers are an easier mark. I cane Mr Butt once or twice in English. Usually I wait until the class have their heads down, and I remark, almost confidentially, to him, 'I'm beginning to enjoy skull again, Mr Butt.'

53

'That's great, Matt. Good for you.'

'The skull day is almost too short, as far as I'm concerned.'

He looks at me. I can hear the hard-drive of his brain clicking away. 'Very good, Matt. Now crack on with your work.'

Debbie Summerhill working at a nearby desk lifts up her head and looks back at me. I would love to ask out Debbie Summerhill. Love it. Love it, love it, love it. But I can't. No. Not with these hands. Though today I have a plan. Today I take her photograph.

Not that she notices, and anyway it's not until the end of History that I get out my digital camera to take a couple of snaps of Druce. He's great. He mugs for the camera, lolls his head this way and that, sticks his fingers up his nose, lets his tongue roll free, all while I snap away. But behind him, just over his shoulder, in focus, where Druce and his arsing around are a bit of a blur, is Debbie.

Gotcha!

She's looking right into the camera and she doesn't even know. Druce doesn't get it either, bless him. I can't wait to get the camera home.

But, as it turns out, Druce walks home from school with me and Mum is there outside our block of flats with her shopping and she invites him up. She likes Druce, Mum does. He goes weird whenever he comes into our house. He turns into this super-polite, ever-so-respectful young man with shining eyes, who minds his 'p's and 'q's and sits bolt upright in a chair. 'Tea? Thank you, Mrs Norris, that's very kind of you, I will have a cup of tea.' And: 'This cake really is delicious Mrs Norris. Did you bake it yourself?'

Bake it yourself? It's that pink-and-yellow-squared stuff that comes with sticky marzipan around it. Who the hell bakes that at home? And he doesn't break it for a second. Nothing I can do can make him snap out of it, either. Not even when I slap his face a little, like you do to bring someone out of unconsciousness. I snort. I laugh. I go, 'Come on, Druce, this is my *mum*! She's not the frigging Queen, for Christ's sake!'

'He's a proper gentleman, Druce is,' says my mum. 'A credit to his mother.'

'Very kind of you to say so,' says Druce, munching his Battenberg cake.

I want to scream. I mean, this is the bloke who gets his todger out and examines it behind the desk at school during Religious Ed.

'How is your mother, Druce?'

'A little under the weather, Mrs Norris. Why, only the other day she . . .'

All this time I'm nursing the camera with the picture of Debbie Summerhill and I want to take it upstairs and transfer it to my computer. But I have to listen to this brain-freezing guff about Druce's mother's varicose veins.

Finally, Mum backs out and lets us go upstairs to my room. Druce immediately starts poking about at all my stuff. He loves my room. He picks up my guitar, twangs it, sets up a game, leaves it, flicks through my graphic novels, tosses them aside. I leave him to it because I'm on my computer, uploading today's snaps.

Druce sees his mug come up on the screen and stands behind me. 'Hey, look at that!' he cackles. 'You've caught Debbie Summerhill in that shot. Why not run Photoshop and stick her head on a nude body?'

'What?' I say. Despite the fact that I spend most of the time imagining Debbie without her clothes, this idea hasn't occurred to me.

'I've always wondered what she'd be like with her kit off,' he drools.

I get up and go to the bedroom door, open it and yell down the stairs. 'Mum, cake-boy here has an idea for tinkering with this photograph. Want to come and watch?'

Druce freaks and slams the door. 'Shut the fuck up!' he goes, his eyes popping. 'What did you do that for?'

'Well, I thought she might want to bring up a bit of that delicious cake and watch us at it.'

'What? You're cracked, you are! Cracked!'

I don't know why it is, but I feel sort of . . . protective towards Debbie. Factoid number twenty-two: not all blokes are pervy about all girls. Deal with it.

Druce picks the guitar off the bed again and vamps out a few duff chords while I finish uploading the photographs. After a few moments he wearily lays the guitar down on the bed and says he should be going.

'See you tomorrow,' I say over my shoulder. Even as I hear his tread on the stairs I'm cutting out Debbie's face and making it into a screen-saver. I hear him exchange a few words with my mum before he leaves.

I shoot off three emails to Jools. One goes: *na na na na na na na na na.* The next reads: *What went ye out of the wilderness to see? A reed shaken with the wind?* I've no idea what that was all about. I think it was something I heard in the church at Jake's funeral, but I didn't realise that until after the email had been sent off, otherwise I wouldn't have sent it. That's emails for you: sometimes they're like arrows that go so deep in the target that you can't pull them out. Anyway, my third one was a direct appeal: *Jools can't you see how it hurts me when you never answer?*

This last email won't make any more difference than that *na na na* rubbish. Nothing works. Nothing.

On the days after Jake appears at the window my body changes. Every time. I don't mean that I turn into a wolf or that I become the Incredible Hulk. That's not what I mean. It's about the way I feel. It's like the blood inside my body slows down. It's like my blood turns to sludge, like old engine oil. Jake showed me how to do an oil change on a car: it's easy. New oil goes in quick, with the light reflecting off it, ready to take any shape it meets. Then when it's been round the engine a good few times it dribbles out like an evil black muddy slop, like a smoker's lungs.

That's how my body feels after Jake has paid one of his night-time visits. And it affects my brain. I feel slow. I feel thick. Plus, I feel edgy. I want to have a go at someone. That's why I pulled up Druce, even though I might have a go at that Photoshop thing with Debbie's head. Then I don't like myself much. Slow and thick. Oozing in his bedroom, a puddle of black oil, this boy.

This has got to stop.

9

The Art of Not Looking

Sarah – and I-praya-to-a-da-saints! – why can't you just shave your legs? It would mean I could look at them again and not feel slightly queasy. In fact, today her bare legs look waxy and shiny, but they still have this ginger stubble growing on them. I wish it wouldn't, but it reminds me of the time I went to a farm on a school visit and stroked a pig. I thought pigs would be smooth, but they're not. They have these bristles. I'm not saying Sarah's legs are the same as a pig's back, but for some reason that's what they bring to mind. I wish I could be more in charge of the things my own mind presents to me.

Today the light from the window ripples across the curve of Sarah's thigh and trickles down her shin. She's crossed her legs again and I wonder if it's really a signal. I mean a come-on. Because if she does fancy me, she's not going to come right out and say it, is she? She'll be scared of rejection. Or maybe afraid I would report her to her senior manager.

And if it really is a come-on, then I would have to break it to her that those legs – which are in every other way gorgeous – are going to have to be shaved before I could even consider it. I'm sorry, but that's just the way it is.

Anyway, I practise the art of not looking at her legs, while she talks at me. This means staring at something on the desk behind her, maybe six inches removed from the hump of her knee, but really you're getting a good eyeful of that one thigh crossed over the other. And I do love the way that the squashy part of her thigh falls over the fleshy bit of her other thigh without sagging, almost as if it has its own air, like a helium balloon, but two days after the funfair. That and the way it makes her toe point towards me.

It's just the ginger stubble that is putting me off.

'Do you think you could look at me occasionally while I'm talking to you?' says Sarah.

Here we go again. So I look at her with eyes wide open. 'Personally,' I say, 'I think this hard-focus eye-contact thing is overrated.'

'Oh, you do? Why is that?'

'Because when you're staring into someone's face it's very distracting from what they're saying. For example, you may notice a small zit on his or her face and once you've seen a zit on someone's face you can't possibly focus on anything else. Factoid number forty-four: zits rule the face, when there is one, I mean. And it's not just zits. What if someone has a twitch. That's hard, when their cheek muscle is flexing all the time or they're nodding their head too much. What are you gonna do? I mean, you can't pretend it's not happening.'

'You've obviously given this a lot of thought.'

'I can give you loads more examples. Have you ever seen a tiny bogey at the end of someone's nostril?'

'I get the picture.'

'Not a complete bogey, just one early in its life, a starter-bogey, where if it was a full one you could say, "Hey, you've got a bogey," but you can't because it's small and –'

'That's enough of that.'

'But you –'

'I said that's enough. I know exactly what you're up to. How is it when I want you to talk about something important you turn into a rag doll, but if I challenge you to stop talking you run away at the mouth?'

'You asked me to talk about eye contact.'

'I asked you to *make* eye contact, not talk nonsense about it.'

'Don't see what the big fuss is about, that's all.'

I say this, and I look away, and though I don't mean to – really, I don't mean to – my gaze settles on the glossy roll of her thigh. The thing is – and I know nobody will believe this – although I *was* looking at her thigh, it wasn't what I was *thinking* about. I was still thinking about this whole business of eye contact.

And Sarah looks at the point of my gaze and then back at me, before uncrossing her legs and tugging down the hem of her skirt. And I blush. I don't mean my cheeks pink up a bit. I mean I feel this angry, hot, purple-red wave start from under my collar and wash right up until my neck is burning, my ears are radiating

61

and my cheeks are flaming. And it's all so bloody unfair! Because I absolutely and categorically was *not* looking!

In a moment of inspirational quick thinking designed to get me out of this boiling, hell-like cauldron of embarrassment I hear myself go, 'There's something embarrassing I have to tell you about.'

She sits upright in her chair. 'Yes?' At least I've distracted her.

'It's about Jake.'

'Yes?'

'Well, it makes me feel embarrassed every time I think about it.'

'I understand that. I understand that these things do make us embarrassed when we talk about them. But I'm hoping that by now you trust me enough to talk to me.'

She's bought it. I sigh, with relief, but that's okay because she thinks it's a sigh of stress. And I tell her about Jake appearing at the window the other night dressed as a girl. I give her plenty of detail. String it out. I have her full attention and I know all that stuff about me looking at her thigh is forgotten.

'It was a dream, Matt.'

'It *wasn't* a dream.'

'Okay, don't shout at me. Even if you weren't asleep, can we at least call it a waking dream?'

'I don't care what you call it. I wasn't asleep.'

'All right. But I think I know the meaning of this waking dream.'

And then she starts talking about the smash. About what she's pieced together from the reports and from the little I've told her. Now she has the eye contact she wants. Laser hot. Melting point. She's got my entire attention. The conversation wasn't meant to go this way, but she tells me what she knows about the moments after the smash. About me trying to get Jools out afterwards, and about me feeling guilty over Jake, and about Jake being her boyfriend, and even though Sarah's being gentle and her voice is low and her eyes are full of sympathy the shaking starts.

The odd thing about the shaking is that I experience it outside my body first, as if there is an earthquake going on. I feel like the room and the table and chairs are shaking. But then it changes and I feel the trembling in my hands. Then it ripples throughout my entire body and I'm shivering like someone with a fever, and my teeth are chattering so hard that they are actually clacking.

Sarah is off her chair and has her hand on my shoulders, either side of my face, and she's asking me a question but I can't hear it. I'm shivering so hard I don't know what she's saying. I can smell her perfume. The scent of her drenches me, but I can't make out her words.

I see Sarah go to the phone on her desk, pick it up and mouth some words into the receiver. Then she comes back to me. After a moment the big, waddling frame of Mrs Took comes through the door carrying a glass of water.

Mrs Took takes over. 'Big breaths,' I hear her say, as if from the top of a mountain, and I remember to breathe. 'That's it, big breaths. Good.'

And after a few moments, the worst of it is over. The shaking stops. I feel sick, but the clacking and the knocking have all died down. It appeared like a sudden hailstorm, and now it has moved on. I'm all right. I tell them I'm fine. I am fine.

'It's a bit warm in here,' Mrs Took says to me. 'Perhaps we need a window open.'

Sarah also thinks this is a good idea. She crosses the room and reaches up to open the small window at the top of the frame. She has to stretch and fiddle with the catch to get the thing open. She's on her toes and her skirt rides up a little, and I think what a great shape she has. So that's it then: 50,000 volts of electricity have just swept through my body, resulting in a shaking fit, I feel like I could puke, but I'm still up for an eyeful of my probation officer's butt.

Factoid number eleven: I'm a perv and no mistake.

Mrs Took follows up her glass of water with a cup of tea. She makes me drink it, even though it must have about six spoonfuls of sugar dunked in it. I say I can't drink it, it's too sweet. I don't do sweet drinks. See that Coke? I never do Coke. If you want to strip the enamel off your teeth, why not just get a pair of pliers or a power tool and just rip it right off in one go? Why mess about over the five years? Why not just drill big holes in your teeth? But anyway Mrs Took sort of bullies me into drinking this disgustingly sweet tea.

I recover quickly and ask them to stop fussing. There is nothing worse than fussing women. Really, I am fine, even though they don't believe me.

'Why do you have to say you're fine when you're so obviously not fine?' says Sarah.

'These young boys,' says Mrs Took, 'they're always after acting so tough.'

I'd like to say something to Mrs Took. A few choice words. But I don't, since she's been so nice with the tea. Instead I give her *the look*. I'm pretty good at *the look*. If you want to know how to do a good look, this is how it goes: first you roll your head back slightly, like you might do if your neck aches a little; then you drop your head forward again, inclining it towards the target (in this case Mrs Took); and then you lift a single eyebrow, really high; keeping both eyes on your target throughout, which goes without saying. That's *the look*. For Frau Took.

'Have you told him about the Programme,' says Mrs Took.

That breaks my look. 'What programme?' I say.

'I'd almost forgotten,' says Sarah, recovering her authority and composure. 'I'll need the papers for his parents' signatures if he's going to be involved.'

'Parents? Signatures? What programme?' I don't like the sound of anything that begins with 'pro' and ends with 'gramme'.

'I'll get them so he can take them home with him,' says Mrs Took and as she turns to leave the room I'm amazed at how vast her backside is, inside this huge floral skirt hanging from her hips like a cloth draped over a dining-room table. It makes me wince. So much so that Sarah thinks I'm wincing at my recent attack of the shakes. I let her think that and tell her I really am okay.

'There's a programme you're eligible for, Matt.'

'No, thanks.'

'If you go on the programme, it reduces your probation time. If I report solid and positive participation, that is.'

I knew it. I knew it all along. I knew they wouldn't let me get away with just coming along here and eye-balling Sarah's legs. 'Let's hear it,' I say, all gloom.

'Should be quite fun, actually. You get to go away for two nights. Almost a holiday.'

'Oh, goodie, goodie! I'll bring my bucket and spade!'

'No, it's not to the seaside. It's at a lodge in the Peak District. You do group sessions, pot-holing, canoeing –'

'What?'

'Yes, it's activity based. Adventure training alongside group discussions.'

'There's no way my dad can afford that lot,' I say. 'He's being made redundant, you know.'

'The probation service bears the cost of all of it. We just need your parents' permission. And your co-operation, of course.'

I sense a trick. I want to say: 'What, the probation service, in recognition of me stealing a car and ruining everyone's life, is going to send me on a canoeing and pot-holing trip? What they gonna do? Cut the rope when I'm halfway down? Hole the boat and push me into the rapids?'

'It will be a good experience for you, Matt. You'll

meet other young people.'

'What about school?'

'Half term.'

'What? I'm supposed to sacrifice my holidays to hang from a rope and put my trust in some kid with convictions for grievous bodily harm? I think not!'

'And how do you think that kid might feel about trusting you?'

That shuts me up for a moment, I must admit. 'Will you be going?'

'No. But my boyfriend Alex is an expert caver and he sometimes leads the outdoor pursuits. He might be there.'

'Great, so I can look at his hairy legs instead of yours,' I very nearly say. But all that came out was 'I dunno. Really, I dunno.'

'Well, I'm not going to twist your arm. I have to admit I'm not sure about your mental fitness for such a trip. I'm not sure you're up to it.'

I'm stung by that. After the burn-out I was examined by a shrink and given a clean bill of mental health, and I say so.

Sarah gets up and opens the door for me, her usual signal that the time is up. 'We'll see,' she says. 'We'll see.'

When I pass through to Mrs Took's reception area I nearly fall over. There she is, just like last time, sitting with her hands in front of her lap. Hairbrush of razor-wire. Doom-curls. And she's only gone and done exactly what I'd suggested as a sick joke.

Mohawk haircut. Thick crest of hair from front to back. Dyed electric blue with orange flashes. Head completely shaved at either side. In fact, just as she'd appeared in my dream. Now that *is* weird. I'm stuck. I can do nothing but stare.

'What you looking at?' she says.

I'm floored. I'm speechless. So Mrs Took fills in the gap for me. 'A cat can look at a queen, can't it, Matt?'

'Be a bad thing, wouldn't it,' says Sarah, catching on, 'if a boy couldn't look at a girl?'

The old bitches are teasing me! What are they saying? That I fancy this little creature of Sauron. 'You must be joking,' I almost shout. 'Not exactly a film star, is she? More like Gollum!'

At that the creature waggles her new Mohawk haircut. 'But Gollum *is* a film star,' she says.

'Ha!' cries Sarah. 'You've got him there, Amy!'

And the three women cackle at me like witches round a big black pot: Mrs Took laughing heartily as she holds out some papers she's just printed off the computer; Sarah throwing her head back; the creature she'd just called Amy giggling uncontrollably.

I grab the papers from Mrs Took, pick up my coat and get out of there pretty damn quick.

10

Keep Your Hands Where I Can See Them

Jools is laughing. In the dark. I like her laugh.

There are all sorts of laughs. Some people have great laughs. Druce, for example, has a laugh that sounds like when you rev the engine on a big motorbike, but then he stops it dead. My dad has a mate from work called Floyd, a guy from Jamaica. He has a laugh so infectious it makes you smile and at the same time makes the hairs on your arms stand on end.

Jools has a laugh that sounds like someone saying, '*Yeh!*' but it takes a long time to come out. You know: '*y-y-y-y-e-ee-ee-eh-eh*'. It's a great laugh. You want to say things to her so you can hear it one more time.

Well, I say Jools *has* a great laugh. Maybe I should say *had* a great laugh. I haven't heard it for so long. I don't know if she still laughs at things. None of us laughs as much as we used to, I guess.

Anyway, she is doing her laugh on this night I'm telling you about, in the dark, in the front seat of the Testarossa, sitting on Jake's lap. After we find the bag of skunk in the glove compartment we have to make a

69

decision. We figure that fatso won't miss his expensive heap until he comes farting out of the restaurant. He'll report it and a description of the car will be flashed through to every patrol car in the area. And this car – the fatmobile, as we've started calling it – does sort of stick out like Prince Charles' ears.

You see the problem, as always, is where to go. When you live at home, that is. You can't just wander in with a bag of skunk and say, 'Hi, Mum, hi, Dad, just nicked this bag of weed from some high-cholesterol fat bastard, and now we're going up to my bedroom to smoke it.' No.

It must be great to have your own gaff.

By the same token we can't just park the fatmobile, skin up and wait for Mr Plod to tap on the window. So Jake remembers the Pikehorn Tunnel.

Doesn't he just.

The Pikehorn Tunnel is part of a disused railway line. The track has all been ripped out, and some years back the old line, including the tunnel, was developed as a cycle path. Then something nasty happened in the tunnel. I can't remember all the details, but someone was murdered, and people stopped using it and it just became a target for vandalism, fires, paint-spray graffiti and the like.

Jake reckons a farmer has taken down a gate at the corner of a field near the tunnel. He thinks you can get the car down on to the old track. His idea is to slip inside the tunnel so that we can sit tight for a bit, then we'll leave the car there and take a bus back into town.

So that's what we do. We switch seats again and I get to have Jools on my lap for a second time.

'Keep your hands off her this time,' growls Jake.

'I didn't touch her!' I protest.

'Keep your hands where I can see 'em,' he says.

'Stop it, you two,' says Jools. 'Matt, you can put your arms round my waist if you like. That's all right.'

'Grrr,' goes Jake.

He drives the fatmobile down to the Pikehorn Tunnel. The road runs parallel to the old railway line, but higher up, on an embankment. There is a fairly steep gradient to get the car down into the field. A few cows graze at the far end of the field, some of them lying down, which I think means they are expecting rain. (I don't know, my name isn't Farmer Giles. Do you see any hay in my mouth? It means *something* anyway.)

Jake makes me get out and go and check the tunnel first, to make sure there are no kids playing round there. The coast is clear, so I wave him in. He brings the car off the road and down the embankment. The Testarossa glides pretty smoothly across the grass, making a kind of whispering as it does so. I get back in, with Jools on my lap again.

'Hurry up,' says Jake, 'we don't want to get spotted.'

He drives right up to the entrance to the tunnel and then rolls the car inside, maybe twenty yards. Jake kills the engine but leaves the headlights on brilliant full beam.

'Spooky,' says Jules.

It is. The full-beam headlamps light up weird-looking, dripping stains on the walls for several yards ahead, but beyond that, nothing.

'Think that's blood on the walls?' says Jake.

'Blood?' asks Jools.

'Yeh,' I say, wanting to scare her a bit. 'Didn't some psycho chop up a woman with an axe in this tunnel.'

Jools looks at Jake.

'Shut up, you tosser!' goes Jake. 'Let's have a go at this weed.' He makes me change seats with him so that Jools is on his lap, and I'm behind the wheel.

Jake rolls the joint. Then he kills the lights and we sit in the dark, passing it back and forth. It isn't good stuff, though. As I've said before, it's too strong, which means you get wasted almost right away. Jake, who knows more about this stuff than me, says that they spoiled it when they started growing stronger and stronger skunk. Killed the art of conversation, he reckons.

Jools thinks it's okay, but Jake is like a connoisseur of fine wines. 'Naw,' he growls, 'this is for zombies. Fatso might have a flash car, but he doesn't know good gear.'

'Unless his girlfriend gives it to him to shut him up,' says Jools.

I'm with Jake. It occurs to me for the first time that perhaps I really don't like the stuff. Any of it, I mean. Maybe I haven't got the right head for it. By the time we've finished the joint between us I'm already wasted. My brain feels like seaweed washing about in a rock pool. I feel like an old biddy on a geriatric ward. My gran had to go and stay in a special old folks' home. I used to visit, but there would be her and four or five other OAPs sitting in the television room watching the box. Only none of them had got up to switch it on. They were all watching the blank screen as if it were showing a news flash. It was weird.

I remember asking my gran if they wanted me to switch it on. She said, 'Can you answer me a question?'

'Yes, Gran.'

'What am I doing here?'

Well, that's how skunk makes me feel. Watching a blank screen but unable to tear myself away. It's supposed to be fun, but it's making me feel sad. Factoid number thirteen: everyone ends up wasted one day.

'You all right, Matt?' I hear Jools say.

'Wasted,' I answer.

'Yeh,' says Jake. 'Me too.'

There's a long pause before Jake snorts. Then he starts tittering, giggling and snorting. And then Jools joins in with her *y-y-y-ye-ye-eh-eh-eh*, and suddenly the pair of them are all over the place, laughing their heads off inside the fatmobile in the dark of the tunnel. It sort of takes over me too, and I'm hooting and howling, but I'm not even sure why I'm laughing.

And it's kind of all right for Jake. I mean, he's sitting there with Jools on his knee and they're laughing and squeezing each other, and when you've got someone like that then it doesn't matter what you're laughing at, does it? I mean, you're just laughing. Who gives a shit? You just hang on to each other and laugh until the snot comes down your nose. But when you don't have someone, well, that's different. Somehow you hear your own laughter kind of cutting back at you. That's how it felt for me anyway, and I really wished I'd got Debbie Summerhill sitting with me, so there could be four of us laughing our stupid heads right off and not caring.

But when the snorting and hooting finally die down Jake gets idea number one. At least I think it was Jake, but what's bothering me is I'm sitting in the driver's seat, not him. He's still got Jools on his lap. No, my memory is faulty: we switch again, that's it. So Jake hotwires the engine again and turns on the lights. 'Let's see how far down this tunnel we can get,' he says from the driver's seat, slipping the car into first gear.

I know the tunnel is about a quarter of a mile long, maybe more, but we don't know if there are any obstructions along the way: old bicycles, bits of chopped-up bodies, stoned teenagers, the usual stuff.

'Go slow,' says Jools.

So we drive pretty slow. There's some fancy graffiti deeper into the tunnel. I mean, really impressive art. Except it would be if it wasn't in a tunnel. The cool thing about graffiti is doing it where you might be caught, not stuffed away in some black hole. I don't know, maybe the artists (and there must have been more than one because the thing is huge) were practising. And it comes alive in the powerful white lights of the Testarossa as we cruise by.

'This painting goes on for ever,' says Jools.

'Yeh,' gasps Jake.

He's crawling now, so we can take in these electric blues, acid yellows, cadmium reds and some of the strange tags up there on the wall. You can make out words but mostly they don't mean anything. The word 'DOOM' keeps coming up, but I don't know whether it's a tag or a message.

Then the graffiti art stops without warning and we're back to the old, stained, damp brickwork. Jake picks up speed, but only a little because there are bits of debris on the track ahead, small stuff that gets crunched under the wheels of the fatmobile.

Then something drags nastily on the front spoiler and buckles underneath in a way that makes us all grit our teeth, but we carry on until we hit a barrier. Jake stops with the headlights beaming on a huge sheet of corrugated metal. It's the other end of the tunnel and it's been blocked.

With the engine ticking over, Jake gets out and gives the metal sheet a kick. It doesn't budge. The smoke from the exhaust, underlit by the car lights, billows around Jake.

'Pretty solid,' says Jake, swinging back behind the wheel.

With only a few feet to spare on either side of the fatmobile, there's nothing for it but to slip into reverse and retreat the way we came. Except Jake thinks it's a wheeze to put his foot down. With only the reversing lights and the red tail-lights to light the way, we fly backwards. After maybe a hundred yards I see an entrance to another passage, a fork in the tunnel, slip by the window. Or at least I think I do, but it's dark and it went by so fast I can't be certain.

I'm just about to mention this to the others when Jake goes, 'Fuck!' and jams on his anchors. The fatmobile squeals in protest and I see out of the rear window that it has stopped just inches from a huge obstacle in our path. The thing is a dark, rusty brown heap. We all get out to take a look.

'This can't be right,' says Jake.

He has stopped the fatmobile just in time. The object is the back end of another car, so the two vehicles are rear bumper to rear bumper. Only this other car is completely burned out. It's a heap of rusting metal and melted plastic and it looks like it's been there a long time.

'But how come we didn't hit it on the way through?' Jools wants to know.

'I don't get it,' says Jake, and for the first time that evening I sense his confidence is gone. Suddenly.

The engine of the fatmobile is still ticking over, and the tunnel is beginning to fill with exhaust fumes. Jake comes round to the rusting burn-out and gives it a push, not that it's going anywhere. And neither, at that moment, are we.

'This can't be right,' says Jake for the second time.

To the Foot of Our Stairs

'How's Sarah?'

'She's fine, Mum. Sarah is fine.'

'Has she got anything to say?'

'Only the usual.'

'What is the usual?' asks Dad.

We're having sausages and mash with onion gravy and peas. I sense there's a bit of an economy drive going on in our house, after the redundancy news, but this is great. I could eat this every night. I could even enjoy it if we didn't have to have all this talking going on. I'm not a great one for talking at the best of times, but this is not even normal talk. It's designed to sound like normal talk, but it's *what's going on in Matt's head* kind of talk.

'This is really great, Mum,' I say.

Mum always smiles when I say that. That's mums for you. You just compliment their cooking and the skin round their eyes goes all crinkly and they smile and they blush a little. They're so easy.

Dad's not having it, though. 'Come on, then. Your mum was asking you about your session with Sarah.'

'No she wasn't.'

Dad drops his knife and leans back from the dinner table; I mean, at a ridiculous angle, as if a sudden high wind has blown him back in his chair. His eyes are splayed open. 'I've just bloody well heard her ask you!'

'She asked me how Sarah was. She said, "How's Sarah?" and I said, "Sarah's fine." That's different.'

'Why have you always got to *come it*, Matt? Why?'

'I'm not coming anything.'

And I don't think I am coming it. I know what I can't say: that all this stuff they are asking me, all this pecking at me over the dinner table, is really about Jake. About how I'm not as good as him. About how I can never fill his boots. About how the best thing I could possibly do now to make up for the crime of not being Jake is to comb my hair and polish my shoes and keep my head down. But I can't say these things over the dinner table or anywhere else. In fact, I can't say much at all, because all conversations lead back to the thing we can't talk about: Jake.

I blame Mum for this. I mean, you don't ask someone how their probation officer is, just like you're asking about your aunt Maggie or your cousin Merlin. (Yes! I've actually got a cousin called Merlin! Can you believe it? His dad is a bird fancier. One of his brothers is called Falcon and his other brother is called Jim because his mum drew the line at Peregrine or Common Bustard or something.) When they say, 'How's Merlin?' you go, 'Fine,' and that's that. They don't really want to know that my nine-year-old cousin

Merlin bought himself a packet of toffees and a *Spiderman* comic from the newsagent today. They don't give a shit about his toffees. So they go, 'How's Merlin?' and you go, 'Fine,' and everyone gets on with their lives. So it's Mum's fault for not being clear.

'You think you're so bloody smart, don't you?' says Dad.

'Stop bickering, you two,' says Mum, coming to my rescue, 'and finish your dinner.'

Dad looks stunned at this remark. 'Well, I'll go to the foot of our stairs!'

That's a good one, that stairs line. It's something he says when he wants to make out that the whole world is mad except for him. I've no idea what the stairs have got to do with the world being insane. One day I'll ask him.

Dad isn't finished. 'You're the one', he says to Mum, 'who says we need to sit at the table like a proper family and talk about things. Then I try to get a peep out of Jimmy Chonga here and you tell me to stop bickering.'

Jimmy Chonga? *Jimmy Chonga?* Who's that? I think my dad makes these things up as he goes along.

'I'm just saying,' says Mum, without saying anything.

But I can see Dad is really annoyed. His fuse is a bit short since they told him they were chucking him out of work, so as a diversionary tactic I remember the forms. The programme. 'I've got some papers from Sarah for you to sign,' I say casually, 'about me going away.'

This shuts them up.

'It's only for two nights,' I say. I get out of my chair and go and fetch the forms from where I'd left them in the hall. I hand them to Dad. 'But you have to give your permission. Both of you.'

Dad looks through the papers with a puzzled expression. It's as if I've been kidnapped and this is a ransom note. Mum gets up and stands behind his chair, reading over his shoulder. 'You didn't tell us anything about this,' says Dad.

'I'm telling you now,' I say, reasonably.

'This is next week?' says Dad. 'Are you ready for this?'

'What's orienteering?' asks Mum.

'Map reading and stuff,' says Dad. 'And they're paying for all of this?'

I shrug.

'What happens if you have a session?' Dad wants to know.

I know he means what happens if I have a screaming fit. A *session* of the blue-blazing, demon-download, full-on freak-out. 'I'll be fine,' I say. 'Really.'

He massages his chin and looks at me like he doubts it.

'You'll have to have a new pair of jeans,' says Mum. 'You can't go with your knees hanging out.'

'I like my knees hanging out,' I say.

Half term rolls around, and though I've signed up and so have Mum and Dad, I'm not sure about this whole deal. First, there's something nasty called *the contract*.

And they want it signed in blood. By which I mean they want your soul.

You have to make a personal pledge. No drink. No drugs. No swearing or abusive language. To co-operate with all rules as laid down by the residential centre. To be in bed with lights out after 10.30 p.m. (Which is hilarious, as I've never been to sleep at that time since I was five years old.) To be out of bed by 8 a.m. Oh yeh, this is a good one: to agree to join group discussions 'in a spirit of openness and honesty'. How are they going to be able to tell what your 'spirit' is? Once, years ago, I nearly joined the Boy Scouts, but I read somewhere that 'a Boy Scout keeps his spirits up and whistles and is cheerful under all circumstances' and I thought, To hell with that. This seems to be the same sort of thing. I wonder if we'll have to sing round a campfire, openly and honestly.

So I have huge doubts about this. But there are the credits. You get credits for your final report and an early signing-off date, so it shortens the period of probation.

Mum and Dad drive me down to the bus station on the Monday morning of half term, where I'm to be picked up by a minibus and driven to the residential centre in the Peak District National Park. Even before I get out of the car I see Sarah leaning back against a bright red minibus.

The words 'Wickhamstead Probation Service' are emblazoned in big white letters on the side of the minibus. Nice. Why don't they just brand us on the face with hot irons, so that everyone can see what we're about?

Sarah is out of her normal probation-office clothes. She looks different in blue jeans and a fleece and for a moment I think she might be going to join us. But no, she's just there to see us off. She shakes hands with my mum and dad, and they go all 'formal informal', swapping unfunny jokes, all big smiles, making remarks *about* me but not *to* me.

'Couldn't you keep him for the full week?' goes my Dad.

'He'll have a great time. He'll be right as ninepence,' says Sarah. 'So long as he doesn't fall down a hole.'

'Can't you sort of put a hole in his way?'

Dad, you are a wag. I'll burst a gut laughing, I will.

The driver of the minibus is a bloke called Bone. A burly old bruiser with a shaved head and a voice box half rotted away from smoking a million cigarettes. He pipes up, 'We've got one or two deep ones all right. Bottomless. We just give 'em a little nudge over the edge if they're too much trouble.'

Laughter all round. Arf arf arf. Pardon me if I chortle into the straps of my backpack.

'Now then,' says Bone to me, but loudly, so that everyone can hear, 'I has to talk to you about phones.'

I want to say, 'Phones, Bone?' but I just say, 'Phones?'

'Yes. Mobile phones.'

'What about mobile phones?'

'You ain't allowed to take 'em with you. So if you have one, you can either give it to me to keep for you, or you can leave it with Mum and Dad. Please yourself which it is.'

This is a turn-up. I don't want to give up my phone. For one thing, how will I be able to text Jools? I've never missed a day. I don't like this at all. 'That's not in the contract,' I say firmly.

Bone claps his huge hands together and goes, 'Haw haw haw! I like it! Ain't you the barrack-room lawyer!' You can hear the tar bubbling in the back of his throat when he laughs. Then he turns to my dad. 'What have you been teaching the lad?'

'Nothing to do with me,' says my dad with a nervous smile.

'I like it, son,' says Bone. Then he steps closer to me and holds out a huge paw. 'Hand it over.'

Everyone is looking at me now: Mum, Sarah, everyone. I take my phone out of my pocket and I give it to Mum.

'Good lad,' says Bone. 'Now, stow your gear in the back, and jump in. There's one more client to come.'

I throw my backpack into the minibus and there she is, looking down her nose at me. Comb of blood. Hairbrush of nails. Her Mohawk haircut is stiff with gel. We both blink. I'm about to climb in when someone taps me on my shoulder.

It's my dad. His hand is held out. He wants to shake my hand. I can't believe that right here, under the steely gaze of the shaved Orc he wants to do the *well now, son* handshake thing. I mean, I don't do handshakes. Ever. They make me cringe. Nor do I do that fake-cool give-me-skin hoopla that teenybopper homeboys go in for all the time. I just don't do any of it, and I certainly do not do hugs. No. But there it is. My dad has his hand outstretched, offered, and he's looking at me with shining eyes. So I take it and then Mum is on me and she's going to smear her lipstick all over my face, so I give her a quick peck on the powdered cheek and turn and get into the van.

While we sit avoiding eye contact a third kid washes up at the bus station. It's another haircut, basically. This kid has his hair spiked down over his eyes and dyed with henna and he has terrible acne. Whoa! There's acne and there's acne. Bone goes through the phone routine with him and he just returns a drippy sort of smile and hands it over all meekly before climbing in the minibus. The kid has nothing to say. Plus, he has a look about him, like someone removed the front part of his brain and he's not sure how or when it happened. I want to cup my hands to my mouth to make a megaphone so I can go, 'Wasted in space!' in a faraway and fading voice. But you don't do that when you've just met someone for the first time.

Well, you can sometimes. So I do: 'Wasted in spaaaaaaaaaaace.'

I'm just doing this when Sarah sticks her head in the bus. 'Matt, you and Amy already know each other. This is Gilbert.'

Gilbert smiles again, even more drippy. No, it's not really a smile. It's more like a little curl at the corner of the lip.

'Are there only three of us?' I ask. Behind my question is, like: is it just me and these two freak shows?

'There were five of you originally,' she says with a smile. 'One got arrested for a serious offence yesterday. The other is a runaway. So, yes, you're going to have the place all to yourselves.'

I look at Amy the Hairpiece of Death and Gilbert the Chin of Boiling Acne. Amy stares dead ahead. Gilbert offers a zombie twitch at the corner of his lip. 'Great,' I say.

Bone jumps into the driver's seat and starts the engine. My folks wave.

Before closing the minibus door Sarah quips, 'I'm sure you'll all be good mates after the first night.'

It's amazing the things people will say when they know you haven't got a gun.

12

The Arse-end of Don't-ever-go-there

'No tins in that bag, Gilbert? None o' your tins, eh?'

This is Bone, mouthing over his shoulder as we shoot north up the motorway, heading for the Peak District. No one has spoken a word since we pulled away from the bus station and I had this strange feeling no one would open their mouth for the entire journey. See how long before you can crack sort of thing. But Bone has broken the nervous silence by yelling at Gilbert.

Gilbert's answer is to make one of those irritating little smiles and to hug his backpack closer to his body.

'No cheeky tins in that backpack, eh, Gilbert?' Bone says again, his voice rasping like a pebble caught under a door. 'No tins. No cans. No colours, eh?'

'Nuff,' says Gilbert. Or I think that's what he says.

''Cos I has to search it, you knows that,' says Bone. 'That's the deal, ain't it, Gilbert?'

Another twitch at the corner of the mouth.

'Only Gilbert likes his tins,' Bone says to us. 'Likes his aerosols, does Gilb.'

The penny drops. Gilbert is a graffiti-goof. A spray-paint splatterpunk. Which explains the bad acne and the dead-fish eyes. He's been sniffing more paint up his nose than he's been slapping on anybody's walls.

Then Amy opens her trap. 'Hey. Are you Gilb?'

The dead-fish eyes brighten a little. He looks at Amy, a little startled at first. Then that smile flickers in the corner of his mouth, before he drops his gaze again and stares at the footwell of the minibus.

'Cool!' says Amy. 'I've seen your tags! Seriously cool!'

I'm not really into that pissing-up-against-a-wall scene but I think I've seen his tag, too. 'Is that, like, the big blue and black numbers?' I ask him.

He doesn't answer. Just stares down into the footwell. So Amy answers for him, but as if I'm slightly stupid and need it spelling out for me: 'Yes, like the BIG BIG BIG black and blue ones! Yep, you could say that! You could!'

I scowl back at her, but now I know I have seen his tag around town. Though, to call it a tag doesn't do it justice. I mean, most graffiti tags are no more than sad, scruffy little bird's nests or fake Oriental squiggles squirted on a wall by some wanker whose balls haven't dropped yet. These things by Gilb are great ballooning murals that must take hours to lay down. I've also thought that they must be the work of a whole painting posse, but no: here I am, in a minibus, looking at Gilb, the most notorious spray-supremo of the entire region, whose work commands respect, dude, etc., whose reputation is awesome, and, well, he's a dork.

What's worse is that Amy is still going, '*Kewl! Kewl!*', and nodding at him under the Mohawk (a haircut I personally went to a lot of trouble to design for her), has gone dewy eyed. I mean, can't she see that the lower half of his face is on fire for Christ's sake? Can't she see that he has the eyes of a rotting halibut? What is it with girls?

'Hey, know that one on the side of the supermarket in town?' says Amy, eyelashes fluttering sickeningly. 'How long did that take you?'

Gilbert – or *Gilb*, as I suppose he would want us to call him – stares back at her like he's looking deep into her soul, which, if you could see Amy's soul, would be a fairground but with the rides going backwards and everyone beheaded and screaming but not out of fun, and instead of coconut shies they'd have human-head shies, yeh, a real horror-bath of a soul, and he goes, in a tiny, dreamy sort of voice: 'Started midnight; finished three twenty-eight a.m.'

'What?' says Amy. 'Three and a half hours? That is wicked!'

I point out that it was actually two minutes short of the full three and a half hours, but they pretend not to hear me.

'What about that one on the underpass, by Regent Circle?'

I can't believe it. This guy's chin is a living science exhibition. Even his zits have zits. But she's leaning forward, pressing her hands on her knees, beaming. Amy Mohawk is falling in love with Interesting Gilbert.

'Two hours straight, then half an hour later to complete,' says Interesting Gilbert.

'That is so wild!'

I don't see much wild about it all. I don't think there's much to it, however big and bold the stuff is. Just to let them know how bored I am with all of this slobbering over a bit of spray paint, I climb over the front seat and talk to Bone instead.

'Buckle yer belt on, son,' he says.

I have a good chat with Bone. When I tell him I'm surprised that the probation service is going to all this trouble just for the three of us, he laughs. I express the view that they must think we're worth it and he laughs again, that little cancer cackle, a bubble of black oil in the back of his throat.

'You're a budget burner, son. That's all.'

I don't know what a budget burner is, so Bone tells me that the probation service – like all local authority services – is budgeted from April to April. Come March, if these departments have any funds left unspent, they run around trying to use up the available money. If they don't, Bone explains, they get less money for next year. So that's where this little number has come from: the inefficiency of the probation office. Money to burn. Kids like us to light the bonfire with.

And there was me thinking they cared about us. Tosser.

Bone falls quiet, so I spend the time watching the oncoming traffic and doing the count when I see a

Subaru Impreza, which is my personal best time. You don't have to start with your best on the count. You just have to get the thing in sequence. But there's not much happening. The best I can manage is a three-car sequence. Every other car on the motorway seems to be a Mondeo and it messes up the count. So I sit back and let the minibus eat up the miles as we shoot through the English Midlands.

Of course, the place is on the edge-of-nowhere in the middle-of-vanishing-point and at the arse-end of don't-ever-go-there. It's called Arnedale Lodge but actually it's a hut in a field. A modern hut, maybe, but still a hut in a field. If any of the kids billeted there had notions about bunking off to the shopping mall or to a club in town or even to the corner shop for ciggies and beer, well, they have that all covered. It's like a vision of life after a nuclear holocaust has ravaged the earth. Moorland as far as the eye can see, north, south, east and west. Grass and scrub and drystone walls. The most exciting thing going on in the entire neighbourhood is the occasional flyover by a pair of sparrows.

We are 'welcomed' by the centre manager, a bloke in a fleece called Pete, and another fat guy with a sweaty, warty face who is dressed in kitchen whites, whom Pete introduces as Cookie. Awww! Nice, eh? Cookie. Yeh. Bone relieves us of our backpacks and makes no secret of emptying and searching them for, well, anything. Meanwhile, Pete, straight into it, no messing, reads us a list of rules. Cookie stands with his fists dug under the rolls of fat lining his hips, studying the three of us closely.

'These in addition to the personal contract you all signed,' says Pete in a bored voice. 'No smoking anywhere on the premises, no alcohol, no drugs obviously, no food other than that supplied by Cookie here, recreation room to be kept tidy, lights out ten-thirty, no moving about the building after that. Any questions?'

'Ten-thirty?' Amy pipes up. 'Are you mad?'

Cookie chortles. Pete says, 'Ten-thirty.'

'What about you,' she counters, 'do you have to go to bed at ten-thirty?'

'You don't seem to realise', Pete says calmly, 'that I'm not on probation. You are.'

In the background is a clattering sound as Bone empties one of our backpacks on to a table.

There's an army feel to the whole thing. It's not prison, but it's not a holiday hotel, either. I am given a room – or more accurately a cell – to share with Interesting Gilbert while Amy is shown to hers.

'Don't we get our own gaff?' I ask.

'No,' says Pete.

'But you're not exactly over-stretched, are you?'

'No, we're not.'

'So why can't we have our own rooms?'

'Sharing is good,' says Pete. There's something creepy about how chilled out Pete is. I wonder if he's one of these Prozac downers we keep hearing about. 'Do you want the top bunk or the bottom?'

'You choose,' I say to Gilbert. He takes the top. I pull

back the sheets on the bottom bunk and I notice this thick rubber sleeve around the mattress. 'No way can I sleep on that,' I say.

'No?' goes Pete. 'Well, I can't stop you sleeping on the floor. Up to you.'

'No way,' I say. 'Why do we have to have these?'

'It's how we keep the mattresses clean.'

I look at Interesting Gilbert, hoping he will back me up. Even though I know he is really listening to all of this, he just stares at the floor.

'I won't get any sleep on that,' I say. 'I'll just have to slit it open and replace it when I leave.'

'If you insist,' says Pete. 'Your parents signed a form agreeing to pay for any damage you do to the property here. Up to you.'

I look at him. He smiles thinly. Bastard.

Bone comes in the room and hands over our backpacks. 'These are clean,' he croaks. 'No tins, no Slim Jims, no matches.'

'Good,' says Pete. 'Now then, you've got twenty minutes to freshen up before lunch. We'll leave you to it.'

Bone and Pete close the door after them. I look at Interesting Gilbert. He stares at the floor again.

13

Do the Old Switcheroo

At lunch (and when I say lunch, I use the term very loosely) I pull the old switcheroo. With some justification, I might add, and not just out of badness.

We are called into the dining room, Amy, Interesting Gilbert and me. Bone is already sitting at a table in his T-shirt, knife and fork at the ready. Lunch is 'served' and he's doing the polite thing, waiting for us to sit down before he tucks in. Pete is fiddling with a drinks machine in the corner while Cookie stands over the table with his big, beefy hands pressed on his mountainous hips. In fact, I haven't seen him move from this position since I got here. Anyway, he stands over the table like that as if expecting everyone to admire his catering work.

And what work it is.

Everyone has the same dish. A grizzled-looking ratburger, with a little puddle of fat in its collapsed centre. Exactly fifteen oven-baked chips (I check the next plate – I'm right, Cookie must have counted them out, fifteen apiece). And this royal feast, this banquet for kings,

93

is garnished with a sprinkling of green plastic-toy frogspawn, which on closer inspection proves to be tiny, bullet-hard peas, boiled to death for God-knows-what crimes against humanity. But let's be fair to the bloke: he has gone to the trouble of putting a bottle of tomato ketchup in the middle of the table. No-effort-spared sort of thing.

Cookie has this smile on his warty face as we all sit down. 'Burger and chips,' he says, as if explaining something written in French on a menu in a posh restaurant. And he shows us his teeth.

Let's just say that you'd need to work a lot of sugar and a lot of nicotine into your teeth to get them into that fine condition.

Pete finishes messing with the drinks machine and comes over to join us. Bone grabs his knife and fork. He looks like a man with a purpose: *kids dumped, lunch going, I'm buggering off early.* That's when I pull the old switcheroo.

'What's the healthy option?' I ask politely.

The switcheroo is a good number. It goes like this: you put yourself in the role of your mum or dad and turn the tables on them. For example, once I was upstairs in my bedroom and I heard Mum and Dad cackling with laughter from downstairs. They had the telly turned up loud. It must have been a good comedy programme because they kept howling with laughter. So I went downstairs and asked them if they wouldn't mind making a bit less noise because I had homework to do.

That's the old switcheroo. Usually everyone is always going on about healthy eating, because teenagers eat crap. So I turn the tables.

There's silence coming back at me, but like a flame-thrower. Cookie knits his brow. He flushes from the neck up. His bottom lip wobbles. 'Burger and chips,' he says. 'All the kids who come 'ere want burger and chips.'

Amy and Interesting Gilbert are blinking at me. I stick to my guns. 'But there *is* a healthy option, isn't there?'

'What do you want?' says Pete.

'Well, something less . . . unhealthy.'

Pete looks at Bone. I notice that Bone has a single eyebrow moving due north. Pete turns to Cookie. 'Have you got any salad, Cookie?'

Cookie shakes his head as if this is the most astonishing and outrageous suggestion anyone has ever made to him in his history as a caterer. 'Well,' he says, like a moody girl, 'I'll have to have a look, won't I?' And off he goes, hands still on his hips.

While he's gone I explain something to the others. 'It was my brother. He worked in a burger joint. He told me if you worked there, you'd never, ever, ever, let another burger anywhere near your mouth. He said the meat was all compressed rubbish and bits of diseased bone and eye and tail with cowshit caked in it, and sometimes it was maggoty and –'

'I think we get the picture,' says Pete.

'Well, it put me off,' I say. 'But don't let me stop you.'

This was all true. Jake had told me that and it did put me off. I know people think teenagers go mad for blob–

95

food, carbs and sugar and crap, but that's because most of us are blobs, isn't it? Why give us a hard time? If we want to blow up like a farmyard oinker that's up to us, isn't it? We don't need exercise, we can get around on fart-gas, so get off our backs, right?

But I stepped off the oinker trail after Jake told me that. I don't want to eat the bull's penis or its bollocks or its tail in a bun, thanks. So I mean what I say. No ratburgers, no glossy bags of shredded-potato-and-fat, no sugar-bombs. None of it.

Cookie comes back with his thumb hooked over the rim of a breakfast bowl. Inside the bowl is a single frigging lettuce leaf, a large one, I kid you not. A lettuce leaf brown at the edge. Oh, and half a tomato hiding underneath it. He sets the bowl down next to my ratburger and chips. Then he steps back, resets his closed fists on his wide, wide hips, and waits for my response.

But it's Amy who bails me out. 'I'm a vegetarian,' she says.

'We want you to be open,' says Pete. 'Open and honest.'

I don't know who this 'we' is that he keeps referring to. Perhaps Pete has got a pet rat in his pocket, but apart from me, Amy and Interesting Gilbert, there's no one else there. Bone, having chomped his ratburger and slurped a mug of milky tea, is already bombing back down the motorway in the minibus. Dear old Cookie is in his kitchen and now and again we get just a hinted report of his mood as we hear the clatter of another giant steel saucepan bouncing off the wall.

Not happy, Cookie. Not happy because when Interesting Gilbert joined Amy in waving the veggie flag it started a rumpus. Pete said if we were veggies we should have ticked a box on the relevant form. None of us had seen a form, we claimed, and I pointed out helpfully that I wasn't a veggie, just someone who had dietary requirements of healthy food. Pete caved in and sent Cookie back into the kitchen to make us all an omelette, which he did. Which is why Pete is now conducting this post-lunch session against a noisy background of stainless-steel pans striking brick in another room.

The room in which we are expected to be 'open and honest' is bare of anything except the moulded-plastic chairs we are sitting on, and more stacked chairs at the edge of the room. The floor is carpeted and everything seems quite new. A panoramic window at one end of the room offers a view across the moor, so we can watch the grass growing while Pete talks.

And, boy, is he a talker.

It's a yak-yak session. He explains to us there will be several yak-yak sessions while we are here: one in the morning, one in the afternoon. But most of the time we'll be following outdoor pursuits. He doesn't call them yak-yak sessions, though.

Open floor, he calls it.

Duh.

Anyway, Pete spends about twenty minutes telling us about his background, how he came to be in the probation service, what he likes about it, what he doesn't like about it. Then he goes, 'Okay, that's enough of me filling the airwaves. Open floor starts now. That means this is your chance to say anything you want about absolutely any subject.'

And then the creep leans back in his chair and suddenly goes silent. And not just for a couple of minutes, either. This guy, who a short while ago couldn't shut his mouth to save his life, has suddenly become one of those monks who go to the top of a mountain and vow never to speak again. And, given the chance to 'say anything we want about absolutely any subject', you can guess what we have to say.

Right.

Nothing.

Interesting Gilbert stares at the cord carpet, fingering his zits. Amy gazes out of the window, hoping for a leaf to blow across the grass and enliven the scene. Silence. Even the thrashing about in the kitchen has stopped.

I look at Pete, but he just gazes dead ahead. The expression on his face is neither friendly nor hostile. You get the impression the bastard has done this before. Well, I'm determined not to be the one who cracks. This is a game I can play as well as anyone.

After maybe ten or twelve minutes Amy sighs heavily and crosses her legs. A couple of minutes later Interesting Gilbert scratches his neck. Pete has turned into a marble statue and this is really beginning to creep me out. No wonder Bone called this a budget burner. I put my hands over my mouth to stifle a huge yawn and as I do so I notice Gilbert's eyes flicker in my direction.

'Why you looking at my hands?' I hear myself saying. The remark pops out of my mouth in a way that surprises even me.

'I wasn't,' says Interesting Gilbert.

'Yes you were.' I hold up my hands, fingers splayed towards him, advertising them to him. 'There you go. No secret. Burned hands, get a good eyeful.'

'He wasn't looking at your hands,' says Amy, diving in, 'any more than you were looking at his chin in the minibus, or any more than you were looking at the cuts and scrapes on my head when we were outside Sarah's office.'

'Hey,' I say. 'Who pulled your pants down? This isn't about you.'

'You're the one waving your hands in the air,' she says. 'You're the one with the issues.'

'What issues?'

She crosses her legs again and looks away. I look to Pete for him to referee this, but he just smiles at me idiotically.

'What issues?' I say again.

'About your hands,' she says.

'I don't have issues about my hands,' I say.

'Yes you do. You always sit with your arms folded so no one can see them. Or you stuff them in your pockets. Like you're hiding them.'

'Rubbish.'

'Let me see them, then.'

I know what she's saying is ridiculous so I hold out my hands for her to see. 'There. What's the big deal?'

To my astonishment, Amy gets out of her chair and comes over and stands in front of me. She takes my hands in hers. Then she kneels in front of me, still holding my hands. She drops my left hand and examines the right, turning it over, looking at the back and at the palm. My skin there is stretched like melted plastic. I've been having physiotherapy to try to get back the full use of my hands. The problem is that I can't fully flex my fingers. It's as if the skin has shrunk and it cramps my hands. It still hurts. It hurts all the time. Only I know how rough it feels.

Amy slowly runs my melted fingers between her thumb and forefinger, each one in turn. I know Pete and Gilbert are watching this, not knowing what to say. Just when I think she's done, Amy looks up at me. The pupils of her eyes are dark and huge and moist. Then she does something weird. She lifts my hands to her mouth and she kisses them. Not just a little peck of a kiss: she actually closes her lips round the knuckles of my fingers. Then she goes back to her seat.

I'm completely freaked out by this. I can't meet anyone's eyes. I have to look away, at the wall, because my own eyes are filling up and I don't want them to see. I don't know what to make of what she just did.

'That's a beautiful thing,' I hear Pete say. 'Beautiful.'

Then I hear him saying, 'Are you all right, Matt? Are you all right?'

I say, 'Yes,' but I know it comes out like a croak.

'Sometimes,' says Pete, 'this job just astonishes me.'

14

Set-up for a Bad Horror Movie

'This can't be right,' says Jake in the dark of the Pikehorn Tunnel.

But I've figured it out. It was while we were reversing, I caught a glimpse. The tunnel splits into two. It's built in the shape of a Y, and as we reversed back we took the wrong fork. That's it. I saw it. But Jake's not having it. He's the kind of guy who doesn't like having simple things explained to him. Jake has to be the face on the case, the man with the plan.

'If there was another fork in the tunnel, we'd see it from the outside,' he says. He's still leaning against the rusting burned-out hulk of the car blocking our way.

'Not necessarily. And anyway, this fork could be very short.'

I can see Jake thinking about it in the dark. Then he reaches into the fatmobile and puts the headlights on full beam. I'm right again: up ahead we can see the brick where this other part of the tunnel ends. Not that it has been blocked off recently. It was originally built like that, maybe to act as a railway siding when they needed to shunt other stuff past.

'See,' I go. 'See.' Somehow brothers get stuck in talking to each other like they're still in primary school.

'He's right,' says Jools. 'But how did they get this car in here? Facing this way? I mean, they couldn't have reversed it in like we did, or it would be pointing the other way.'

The three of us stand around for a minute, trying to work out the puzzle. Then Jake goes, 'Who the hell cares? Come on, if we retrace our path we should get back on to the main line. Then we can reverse out the way we came in.'

So we all climb back into the fatmobile. Jake takes the wheel, I'm in the passenger seat and Jools squashes on my lap again. I just love the way she smells. It's not just the perfume she's wearing; it's her skin. I'll bet you could get twenty other girls to wear the same perfume from the same bottle and they wouldn't smell as good as Jools does. Plus, she's wearing the new leather coat she's been given for her seventeenth birthday and the smell of the new leather and of her skin and of her perfume is driving me crazy. I decide that if I ever do manage to find myself a girlfriend, she has to smell exactly like that: of leather and skin and Jools' perfume.

Jake drives forward, leaving the rusting hulk behind us, and sure enough we find the place where the tunnel forks. We shoot back out on to the main track, Jake stops, slips the fatmobile into reverse and suddenly boots the accelerator.

'Hey!' Jools and I go at the same time as the Testarossa roars backwards through the tunnel. I don't mind, as Jools spills all over me. As she's tipped forward, she tries to grab me to steady herself, and she accidentally grabs my crotch.

I gasp, but I say nothing. Then she grabs the collar of my jacket. I don't know if she knows what she did. If she does, she's not saying anything either.

Jake slows down. 'Let's try something,' he says, and he kills the lights so now we're cruising along slowly in reverse, but in pitch darkness. The passenger-side rear wheel bumps against something in the dark, maybe a brick.

'Put the lights back on,' says Jools. 'This is creepy.'

Jake ignores her and we're moving like a needle through a lake of black oil. Then the rear wing scrapes, just a little. Jake corrects his steering and giggles. I open the glove compartment and the tiny bulb in there underlights our faces, like in a crappy horror movie.

And it *is* creepy. We can't see anything outside the car. Inside, I see Jools' eyes and Jake's eyes, wide open, black and bulging, shining from the glove compartment underlight. Then there's a speck of light ahead as we see the road lights near the tunnel entrance and Jake takes that as his cue to increase the speed.

We come shooting backwards out of the tunnel like a bullet, but then Jake steps on the brakes. There's a brief skid. He finds first gear and returns just inside the tunnel.

'What is it?' says Jools.

'Someone up there. On the grass bank.'

I look across the field. There is a man there, looking back, maybe towards us. At first I think he's clocked us. He's peering our way. Then I decide he's just waiting for his dog. The dog runs towards him and the man walks away, raising his arm so that the dog jumps for a stick or some other object in his hand.

'Did he see us?'

'Nah. Don't think so,' I say. 'Just some old bloke exercising his mutt.'

'One last smoke,' says Jake.

'We'd better go now,' says Jools.

'I promise you,' answers Jake, already skinning up. 'One last smoke and that's it.'

15

A Brief Introduction to Equestrianism

'Horses? No one said anything about horses!'

We are surprised when the Arnedale Lodge minibus pulls up in a stable yard. I don't know why we're surprised, because when asked where we were going all Pete would say was 'It's a surprise.' I don't know why people say this. Telling people they've got a surprise coming should remove the element of surprise. But it doesn't.

Because horses were not exactly what I was expecting. There is a row of stables with the animals sticking their noses over the doors. A pitchfork rests against a fence. There's a lot of hay and the smell of horse-shit in the air.

Pete ignores my remarks and climbs out of the driver's seat. 'Jump out, guys!' he yells as he saunters across the yard to speak to a woman carrying a saddle.

'Horses!' says Amy, and she's out of the door. 'That's cool.'

Interesting Gilbert strokes his wild chin. He looks like he's on my side about this one. I mean, I thought we were going abseiling, or caving, or on some similar test-of-character activity. I didn't sign up to spend an afternoon playing My Little Pony.

The woman dumps the saddle over a stable door and crosses the yard to greet us. She doesn't smile. In fact, the expression on her chops suggests she might be doing us all a big favour. Come to think of it, she has a face like a horse: long, and a pursed mouth. I wonder if spending too much time around horses can make you look like one. I'm not joking: once I saw a fishmonger who looked like a fish.

'This is Zoë,' says Pete. 'Listen to what she tells you.'

There's no 'Hello', 'How are you?' or any of that. No kiss-your-arse. It's straight to it. Zoë could clearly do with a course in good manners. She's got a head of curly red hair and she tosses it like a horse's mane. Her skin is weathered, like she spends every single day of her life on the back of a horse. She's about the same age as Sarah, but not quite so pretty. A pair of dungy jodhpurs are stretched tight across her crotch and arse. 'We're not hanging about,' she says, and she has this weird way of baring her teeth when she talks. 'We're trekking nine miles and it's going to rain later. We've got to be back here before we get wet.'

'Why not just stay indoors,' I suggest. 'Reduce the risk.'

Zoë doesn't smile or even answer. But I see a scary light go on in her eyes. She regards me steadily. She tosses her head again, and bares her teeth. 'Who has ridden before?'

'I have,' says Amy. 'Couple of times.'

'I'll lead, you go last. Amy, is it? Is that okay, Amy?'

'Fine.'

'Hold on,' I say. 'I'm not going anywhere on a horse.'

'Scared?' says Zoë, and there's that light again in her eyes. 'Boys are always scared around horses.'

'It just doesn't interest me.' I look to Gilbert for support but he's doing his usual trick of staring down, this time at a small pile of dung on the ground. I can see his eyebrows knitting, and I know he's not up for horsey-horsey any more than I am.

'What about you?' Zoë asks Gilbert. 'You scared too?'

Gilbert mutters something. No one quite hears. Zoë asks him what he said and he mutters something like, 'I'll give it a go.'

Wimp.

'Just you then,' says Zoë. 'That's all right by me because I don't want anyone on one of my horses who doesn't want to be there. You'll be on what Pete calls the Alternative Programme. Right, Pete?'

Pete, who has been watching this exchange with a fascinated smirk, says, 'Absolutely right.'

I don't like the sound of this, and when Zoë strides away and commands me to follow I walk behind her. I don't fancy her or anything like that, but I can't seem to keep my eyes off her swinging bottom stuffed into those tight jodhpurs. We walk towards one of the empty stables. She opens a door. Inside there's a messy pile of straw and there is horse-shit everywhere. Tons of it. There is also a wheelbarrow, and a pitchfork.

'Well?' she says.

'Well what?'

'That shit, that wheelbarrow,' she says, and then she swings around and points to a pile of compost in a nearby field, 'that dung heap.'

I get it. She looks at me, and there's that light in her eyes again and I can tell the bitch is having a good time at my expense. Zoë bares her upper lip at me. I can't help it: I'm the one who blinks first. That's all it takes, a blink. She turns around and walks away, and without even looking back at me she yells out to Pete, 'He's coming with us.'

Moments later we all have our riding hats crammed on our heads, Pete included, and we all look like tossers. Hey, that's flattened the Mohawk, I want to say to Amy, but she's been given the prefect's badge by being allowed to ride at the back, so she's still glowing at the thought of her superiority. Gilbert looks like he wants to escape and hide inside a can of spray paint. Then Zoë has a scrawny stable-girl trot out our horses.

The scrawny kid gives Pete a chestnut called Mincer or Ninja or Pincher, I don't know.

Then Zoë looks at me and I don't know if she's kidding, but she says, 'He's a big lad – give him Lucifer.'

Lucifer? Lucifer! Out comes this dapple-grey thing that is as big as a house. I'm going to need a stepladder to get on it. It keeps flicking back its head, and then it turns in a circle and stamps, really hard, almost kicking a hole in the concrete. *Clack!* The steel of its shoe rings on the hard surface. Plus, it has a weird eye, like more white than black. I don't like this horse at all. 'Can't I have one that's been tamed?' I say.

'He'll settle once you're on 'is back,' says the stable girl – a real yokel she is – and she trots mad-eyed Lucifer the psycho-stallion across the yard to me. Maybe I imagine it, but I think I see flinty sparks as its hooves strike the concrete. The girl holds out the reins, but I'm not going near the deranged creature. I can tell it's going to bolt at any moment. It's like something ridden by the Horseman of Death at the very end of the world.

'You must be joking!' I say.

Amy steps across, takes the reins from the girl and starts patting the brute and scratching its head. The animal dips its head into Amy's shoulder and nuzzles up against her. She blows a stream of air near its mouth. The creature seems to like it. I take a step closer. It snorts loudly and I jump back.

Zoë comes up behind me. She takes the reins from Amy and arranges them in my hands. 'When you're up there, this is how you hold the reins.' She folds the leather into my hands, under my thumbs. Though she can't help noticing, she says nothing about the state of my hands. I explain to her that I have no feeling in my thumbs. 'How about here?' she says, pinching between my fingers. 'There? Okay? Well, you'll have to fold the reins there, because you need to feel the pull on his mouth. Lucifer needs only the gentlest touch. If you pull too hard, he'll fight you, and he'll win. You know how to be gentle, don't you?'

And the females all look at me – the stable girl, Zoë, Amy – all waiting to see if I answer the question correctly.

'What about that mad eye?' I ask. 'I think it's got rabies.'

Zoë laughs for the first time, and Lucifer snorts along with her. 'It's a wall-eye,' says Zoë. 'It means nothing.' She cradles her hands together and offers me a foot-up so I can climb into the stirrup. 'Well? Are you getting on?'

I swing up into the saddle, and as I do so Lucifer spins round until Zoë grabs his bit. Then he stands still, and he stays that way until all the other riders are mounted. It seems a long way to the ground. We're not moving but I'm gripping like mad with my knees because I know this bastard horse is going to leap the fence or rear in the air at any moment, and just for laughs.

Meanwhile, Interesting Gilbert gets a black thing called Shandy, Pete has Mincer and Amy leaps up on to another chestnut called Scooter. I'm not making up this shit.

Scooter!

'Lucifer's mah favourite,' the scrawny stable-girl tells me. 'Really fast, 'e is.' It doesn't help me one bit, knowing that.

Zoë has this really fancy-looking bay horse, the colour of sand, all neatly trimmed. She leads, and everyone else trots behind as if they know their exact place in the line. When I finally let myself breathe, all I can smell is saddle leather and horse. It fills my nostrils. The horses walk steadily up an incline before passing between some drystone walling into open moorland. Everything seems to be okay and then Gilb's horse in front of me drops dung right in our path. I have to look at the stuff squeezing out of the horse's arse. I tell you, horses are dirty bastards.

We wind our way along a stony path and then we go up a hill so steep I have to lean forward. It's a strange thing, but as I feel myself relaxing, I feel the horse relaxing, too. As the tension goes out of me, it goes out of the horse. How can that be? When it stumbles I clench up again and I feel the horse tense up. I breathe out, it breathes out. Somehow we're together. Me 'n' Lucifer.

Up and away we go, on to a high ridge, down the other side, alongside a cascading stream, before we splash on through. Then we cross in front of an abandoned mill and our horses' hooves strike on the flinty ground. The amazing thing is we don't see another human being for almost the entire ride. I didn't know there were still places like that in England. I feel like an American Indian winding through the land. For one daft moment I almost want to get myself a Mohawk like Amy's. I nearly say something about it to her but instead I hear myself go, 'You all right, Gilbert?'

'Yeh,' he goes, 'I'm all right.'

I hear Amy behind me. 'You all right, Matt?'

'Yeh, I'm all right.'

'That's good then,' says Amy. 'We're all all right.'

After an hour or so, we drop into a valley, wind our way through and come out on a gentle slope of open moor. Zoë pulls up her lead horse and all the other horses stop dead. 'Everyone still here?' she says.

I pat my horse. 'Easier than I thought,' I say, beaming brightly at her, standing in my stirrups just to give my arse a moment's relief from the saddle.

It's absolutely the wrong thing to say to Zoë. That weird light goes on in her eye again. She looks over to Pete. 'Insurance up to date?'

'Oh, bloody hell,' says Pete.

'Who's ready to let 'em go?' asks Zoë.

'Me!' says Amy.

'Don't, Zoë,' says Pete. But I see he's already gathering up his reins.

I know exactly what's about to happen. Somehow Lucifer is already bristling and telling me. 'What if we fall off?' I ask.

Her horse knows it, too. It's circling, biting at the bit. 'No, don't fall off,' she says.

'Right. Thanks.'

'Better not,' Pete tries again, but it's useless against this woman. 'Oh, bugger!'

'If you get into trouble,' yells Zoë, 'just grab the horse's mane and hold on tight.'

She gives us no more time to think about it. She flicks her horse on and the next thing I know Lucifer and all the others are at the gallop and my arse is polishing the saddle. The horses are going hell for leather, they're actually racing, and I tell you Lucifer just *flies* to the front with no encouragement from me. I'm losing my seat so I grab Lucifer's mane and hang on grimly. Zoë's bay tries to keep pace but it just hasn't got the speed of my horse and all I can hear is the pounding of hooves behind me and the banging my heart is making trying to get out of my ribcage.

The speed is incredible. A good motor has grunt. This animal has *grunt plus*.

I don't have to do anything. Lucifer takes over and gallops up the steady incline. I've no idea what's at the top and whether I'll get thrown over some ridge, but you know what? I don't even care. The horse is in control and I've signed myself over. It races to the top and, in its own time, it slows, steadies and turns gently before stopping. The other horses come thundering up behind, and taking their lead from my horse they all come to a stop in the same place.

My hands are trembling. The horses stand, blowing and breathing hard. When I finally manage to let go of the reins I unclench my fists and take my knees off the horse's flanks. I start giggling like an idiot. Gilbert is laughing like a maniac, too.

Pete is laughing and trying to catch his breath. 'You'll get me fired!' he's telling Zoë. 'You will. You'll get me shot.'

Amy looks deliriously happy. She pats her horse and then she points at me. 'Look at him,' she shouts. 'He won't admit it, but he fuckin' loves it!'

Zoë turns her gaze on me. That light is on in her eye. She doesn't say anything.

16

Your Basic 'Don't Go There' Deal

Back at Arnedale Lodge, ten-thirty approaches and they're serious about this lights-out thing. Maybe they should call this joint the Arnedale Young Offenders' Home or even the Arnedale Bang-up. It's more like a prison than the leisure centre we were promised. I mean what does the word 'lodge' conjure up? Some place with a big roaring log fire, deer antlers mounted on the walls, animal skins for carpets; a place where you relax drinking beer or wine in front of the fire until the wee small hours. Maybe a hot-tub you can all sit in and party.

Not this place, with its arse-numbing plastic chairs and stinky rubber covers on the mattresses, and lights-out in the middle of the day.

Plus, what bugs me is that when the day went so well with the horse-riding, everyone was all smiles. All pals together. Later no one complained about the really duff cheese salad Cookie laid before us: block of rubberised Cheddar, one large, limp lettuce leaf, one tasteless tomato, one dodgy dollop of pickle, and fifteen (yes, I counted them again, out loud this time) chips. No, we ate with cheerful faces, I kid you not, and do we get any reward? Like being treated as adults and being allowed to go to bed when we're tired?

The evening had been wasted with another yak-yak session with Pete. We talked about the horse-riding and what we got from it. I said I got a sore thigh where the saddle rubbed against the seam of my jeans. That and a slightly aching butt. Okay, it was a horse ride. It wasn't *that* great. Though, to listen to Pete, it sounded like he wanted it to be a life-changing experience. I mean, it takes more than that. You can't just take a kid like Amy or Interesting Gilbert and stick them on the back of a horse in the middle of nowhere and expect them miraculously to transform into a normal human being.

Yak-yak takes us up to nine-thirty, then Pete tells us we have an hour of 'free association'. This means we can do what we want, apparently. So what happens? We stay in the same room, still talking about horses. Or at least the others do. I'm certainly not going to waste my free-association time like that, so I wander out into the hall and read the noticeboard. Something about badgers and the environment. Something about a bat watch. Well, that sums it up around here: hey, let's have a big party night and watch a bat!

The doors are very locked. I wander back into the room and, for God's sake, they're still talking about the same sodding thing! 'Look!' I say. 'This is free-association time! Horses is done!'

Pete remembers that we're allowed a bedtime drink. He offers us a choice of hot chocolate or Horlicks or warm milk. Pardon me! I forgot to bring my teddy bear!

'Do we get a bedtime sto-wee?' I ask Pete in a tiny voice.

He sighs a big deep sigh, like he's really tired now. 'You want a drink or not?'

I go for the chocolate. We all do. 'Thought you were vegetarians,' I say.

'Uh?' goes Amy.

'It's a joke!' I almost scream. 'Does a sense of humour go out with the lights here or what?'

'Funny boy,' says Amy. 'Know what? You're funny like having head lice is funny.'

Interesting Gilbert smirks and sips his chocolate.

I ask you.

So we're stuffed into our cell-like rooms, lying in the dark on sheets which slide about on the rubber sheath over the mattress. Even the lights are centrally controlled. I know because I tried switching the light back on, but it was dead.

It's ridiculous. We're wide awake. I never sleep before midnight. Even that would be an early night for me. It's just the way I'm made. I'm a night owl. Some people are up with the lark. But you shouldn't try to turn owls into larks. It's completely against nature.

I run this idea past Interesting Gilbert. From his bunk, in the dark, he agrees with me. I ask him if he is an owl or a lark.

116

'Dunno,' he sniffs.

Christ, what a conversationalist. Interesting Gilbert has so much to say for himself you could write it on the back of a postage stamp and still have room for a shopping list. Maybe he's a brain-weak text-head. One of those kids who can only think and write in text messages. *Where r u? Spk 2 me. Say sthg! R u Dead? How wd u no?*

All *I* know is I'm not going to get much chat out of him. I swing out of bed. 'Come on,' I say, 'let's visit Amy.'

At least he doesn't need much persuading. We pull blankets over our shoulders and, since we're not actually locked in the cell, we can get out into the hall. Amy's room is just across from ours, and I tap gently on the door. She doesn't answer so I knock a bit harder.

I hear a thump, then she comes to the door but doesn't open it. 'Who is it?'

'Keep your voice down, Amy! It's me and Gilb.'

'What do you want?'

'We want to talk.'

'What about?'

'Anything. Anything at all.'

'I'm not snogging you. Either of you.'

Hell, what is it about girls? You want to talk sensibly to them and they think you just can't wait to stick your tongue down their throats! When, to be honest, you'd rather stick your tongue into the moving parts of a waste-disposal unit. 'We can't sleep! We want to talk!'

She opens the door a crack. She eyes me suspiciously, then looks at Gilbert behind me. Finally, she lets us in and closes the door behind her. There are two pairs of bunk beds in her room. Amy scampers back under the covers of her lower bunk and Gilbert and I park ourselves on the second lower bunk just across from her, but not before I open the curtains. The night sky outside looks clear and cold and there is enough moonlight streaming through the window for us to see each other.

'You're not staying,' says Amy, 'if you're going to be Mister-I-hate-everybody.'

She's looking directly at me. 'That's not what I am,' I protest. I look at Gilbert.

He shrugs. 'You are. Kind of,' he says.

Oh? Where did he suddenly get an opinion from? I'm a bit hurt by this. That's not how I see myself. But I don't argue. We start talking in low voices, about Pete and Cookie and this place where we've all washed up. I say something that makes Amy giggle and she has to put her hand over her mouth. She has a good giggle. I like it. Gilbert goes, 'Shush! We don't want to get caught.' Amy grabs the blanket off her bunk, flings it round herself and comes across to our bunk. She takes one end of the bunk and Gilbert and I squash up to the other end.

The talking and the giggling go on well into the night.

And all this stuff comes out, about why each of us ended up there. Amy is the one who opens it up. Turns out she's an arsonist, though she admits she didn't even know what one was until she had to go to court one day. The word 'arsonist' still makes her giggle.

And I do love that giggle of hers. It's not like Jools' laugh. It's different. Listening to Amy giggle is like having someone tickle you. It makes me want to hear it all the time. Except that it's not really funny, her story. She's a fire-starter all right. Seems like she can't stop herself sometimes. That's what she says, anyway. She says she gets way depressed and if there are matches or a lighter around, well, you'd better watch out.

I want to ask her why she does it, but the question would be stupid. Just as stupid as asking me why my dead brother keeps paying me visits in the middle of the night. And if I ask her, then she can ask me, and even if I want to answer that question, I know that I can't. Just like I can't quite remember everything that happened in the tunnel. So it's a *don't go there* deal.

'Suddenly I'm glad we're not allowed to smoke in here,' says Gilbert, and that makes her laugh, too.

He's coming out of himself, is Gilbert. He's like a tortoise with his neck pulled in and now he's just beginning to push it out again. Man, he is one hell of a tag-head. He's a loner, we find out, a complete one-man show. He's got no friends, no posse; he's just out there in the night spraying out his monster tags.

When Gilbert first got caught doing the side of a train carriage he was given a community service order. He was sent round to an old lady's house, to cut the grass and do odd jobs. While the supervisor was away the old lady asked him to do a little painting job and he was slapping white emulsion on the wall when she asked him what his offence was, what with him being such a nice, quiet, obliging boy. He told her, and the next day he took in some photographs of his work to show her. She said she thought they looked very jazzy and could he do her spare room like that? So that's what he did, and she was so pleased she asked him to do the main bedroom, too.

The supervisor turned up and freaked out when he saw Gilbert's tags all over the house. It turned out the old lady was partially sighted and they thought Gilbert had done this out of badness. Gilbert was marched back to court and they sent him away to a young offenders' centre for a whole year.

'There was one kid who'd beaten up an eighty-two-year-old lady. A real scumbag,' says Gilbert. 'He got six months for that. I got a year for painting a room.'

It's a terrible story. Amy and I stare at him in silence.

Then Amy says, 'It wasn't your fault the old lady was half blind.'

'No,' says Gilbert. 'Not my fault at all.'

Then we all get the giggles so bad we have to stuff the corners of the blankets in our mouths so that we won't howl the place down and get caught out of bed. I'm laughing so much I have snot coming down my nose.

When the snorting and giggling stop Amy says, 'What about you?'

I tell them about Jake being killed and about Jools wrecking her face. I tell them what I can remember about the tunnel, or at least the things leading up to the moment when it all goes black. I don't tell them about

Jake visiting me in the night. They don't need to know about that.

I get up and look out of the window, at the moonlit moorland stretching away for miles. I can see the craggy top of a hill gleaming under the moonlight. Something swoops across the land, not far from the house, and I wonder if Jake is out there in the night. I wonder if he's followed me all this way.

Then there is a thump from another part of the building, and a light goes on somewhere.

'Better go, eh?' says Amy.

'Yeh,' I say. 'Better had.'

Gilbert hands me my blanket and Amy opens the door for us.

'Night, Amy,' I say.

'Night, Matt,' she says. 'Night, Gilbert.'

17

What the Mist Tells You about Everything

We turn in and pretty soon from the bunk above me I can hear Gilbert's breathing change as he falls asleep. He smacks his lips a bit in his sleep and I think I hear him murmur a girl's name. Or maybe he's just dreaming about spraying his tag on the sky. You do wonder about some people's dreams. Like Amy: I wonder if in her dreams she's still trying to light fires or whether she's running around trying to put them out.

But I can't dream because I can't sleep. I lie awake for a while. For one thing this rubber envelope under the sheet makes it impossible to get comfortable. I've heard of people who get turned on by rubber. Pervy types. I don't get it. It's so uncomfortable I have to remake my bed. I take a spare blanket from the wardrobe, rip off the sheet and pack the blanket over the rubber. Then I put back the sheet. Gilbert snoozes on. When I climb back in bed it almost feels worse: the blanket beneath the sheet rucks up. But at least I don't have to squeak about on the rubber.

So I lie there, staring into the dark, thinking about

the day. A lot happened. I got to meet Amy and Gilb, who I have to say are pretty cool. I had my first horse ride.

Moonlight streams through the gap in the curtain, and it is actually coming in like rays in a drawing of moonlight. I get up again and look out of the window. There's a mist out there now, but just on half of the moor, as if it rolled along so far and suddenly decided to stop. I don't understand the countryside. It's full of mystery.

'Gilbert,' I whisper, 'look at that mist!'

He makes a snorting noise and smacks his lips again in his sleep. I decide not to wake him. Though maybe I should, because this mist is in no way ordinary. Like I say, it has stopped dead, dividing the moor with a clean line. The moon shines down across the craggy hills and the stumps of trees and gorse bushes on one side, and over this mist it ripples like silver water.

Then I think I see things swimming inside the mist itself, like coloured fish. Brilliant colours, like flashing banners of crimson and yellow and turquoise, they swirl around inside the mist like silk in a tumble dryer. And as I watch this the mist gets whiter, brighter and it starts to roll up towards the window. I look for some way to open the window, but of course I can't. The window catches are designed so that you can't get them open more than an inch, and I remember that I'm locked in.

The colours flashing inside the white mist are beautiful. As it swirls nearer I realise the colours are not *like* silk, they *are* silks, those shirts that jockeys wear, all rippling now under moonlight, each belonging to a different jockey riding about inside the mist. Then one of them, in silks of royal blue and yellow quarters with a blue cap, comes riding towards me.

The jockey is riding that special bay, Zoë's horse from the stables. But its feet aren't touching the ground, and though the jockey is riding hard, hunkered down, flicking the horse's flanks with his whip, the horse doesn't seem to get much nearer to me, and I'm not sure I want it to.

'Gilbert!' I whisper. 'Gilbert!'

He doesn't stir. I fiddle again with the aluminium window fastener, but I can't get the window open more than a fraction. Instead, I press my face to the glass, to see better. The jockey is still riding hard towards me, slapping the flanks of his horse with that vicious leather crop, and maybe he's making progress now, maybe an inch or two, but no more. I don't recognise the jockey. He's got his cap pulled down and he's wearing goggles like they do in the Grand National. I can hear the hooves drumming even though I know they're not connecting with the earth. Bloody hell, the horse is maybe five or six feet in the air and still riding hard out of the mist. Then I figure out that it's the mist that's pulling him back.

I let go a big sigh and it's incredible but my sigh forms into a misshapen bubble. I can see it: a silver, jelly-like thing, this sigh, streaked with rainbow colours where the moonlight strikes it. It passes clean through the glass, spreading as it goes and blowing back the mist outside. I'm so astonished by this that I purse my lips, and I blow, not a big huff and puff, just a little stream of air like you might blow to cool your soup. I'm even more amazed to see another bubble come out of my mouth, pass through the glass and roll back the mist for hundreds of yards.

What's more, it allows the horse and jockey to break free and suddenly they are rushing towards me at terrifying speed, big and scary, hooves thundering against the ground. Then they are right on me, right outside the window, rearing up, the horse thrashing its legs at me. And the jockey is Jake. Of course it's Jake! I knew all along it was Jake. And his face is like rubber as he thrashes the horse and twists his mouth at me.

'What are you doing, Matt?' he yells. 'What the hell are you doing?'

'I'm not doing anything!'

'What the hell are you playing at?'

But I can't answer and the horse rears again, smashes at the glass with a hoof and somehow gets its huge head right inside the tiny crack of the open window. It has a wall-eye and its teeth are yellow and dripping slime and biting at me. The horse bites my hand, shredding the skin, and I'm screaming at Jake to leave me alone. Screaming and screaming.

The horse is halfway inside the room with its hooves on my chest and I'm pinned down and I can hardly breathe. I'm still screaming, and then Jake's voice turns into Pete's voice and I'm on my knees on the bed and he's talking to me in a calm voice: 'Matt. You're okay, Matt. Do you know where you are, Matt?'

I look behind him. Gilbert is there, shivering, blanket over his shoulder, fingering the acne explosions of his bad, bad chin. And there at the door is Amy, burning me with her eyes. They're all watching me.

I look at my hand where the horse bit me. It's all cut. My breathing starts to return to normal.

'That's better,' says Pete. 'That's better.' He looks at the window. Though the glass is intact, there is blood on the metal window lock. 'Don't worry about that,' he says. 'Let's attend to your hand.'

'It's nothing. I'm all right now,' I say. 'Thanks. I'm okay. You can all go back to bed.'

'You want to talk for a while?' Pete asks me. He looks concerned.

'No. Everyone can go back to sleep. It never happens more than once in a night.'

This is true, but I'm desperate to get rid of them. I don't want all this attention. The truth is I'm embarrassed as hell. Not about the screaming, though that's bad enough. It's something else. I'm sitting on a warm wet patch, and I don't want Pete or any of the others to see.

Now I know why the mattresses have rubber covers.

18

Laughing Makes Your Nose Run

So we're in the rabbit hole, like in *Alice in Wonderland*. Or rather, the tunnel, the Pikehorn Tunnel, but it starts to feel like *Alice in Wonderland* because Jake rolls another of these smoky skunky stinkies and it's too strong.

I mean, it's just too strong.

And here's where things get a bit hazy. I can't quite remember the order of things. Up to this point it's all clear, but then I get really out of it. I remember Jake passing me the joint and the word from the tunnel graffiti ringing in my head like a funeral bell: 'Doom. Doom. Doom.'

Is Jake in the driver's seat or is it me? If I'm in the passenger seat, then I have Jools on my knee, feeling her gentle weight shifting on my lap, breathing the sweet smell of her, her perfume, the shampoo in her hair, her new leather coat. And though I'm too far gone to speak, I know that Jake is the luckiest guy in the world.

It seems to me that Jools is perfect. Everything about her. It's like she was dropped on this earth wrapped in cellophane. Really, she doesn't have a single flaw; not one that I can see, anyway. If I look into her dark brown eyes, she seems to understand me without me having to say anything. Her smile takes my breath away. She has great style, Jools does. She looks like a model, except she doesn't have the cat's-arse smile on her face that models go for.

I don't know how she does it, but there's a neatness about her. She can rough and tumble with anyone, but there's never a hair out of place. She's one of the few people I know who can wear white trousers. See, if that were me, or Jake, or probably even Debbie Summerhill, and we wore white trousers, I can guarantee that within five minutes of pulling them on there would be tomato sauce or grease patches or mud splatters all over them. But Jools comes in this glossy, waxy wrapping that resists all stains and all creases.

If Jools wasn't my brother's girlfriend, there would be a strong chance that I would fancy her.

It's a good thing for Jake that it's me in the passenger seat with Jools on my lap. I mean, if it had been anyone else, any other guy, maybe Jake wouldn't have trusted them. I remember thinking it's lucky for Jake. But at the same time a brilliant thought strikes me about that other wrecked car. The one in the tunnel. The burned-out wreck in the siding. We couldn't figure out how it got there, pointing forward. But I see it clearly.

The thing is, I'm so out of it I can't get my words out to explain. I try to demonstrate with my hands, but because I can barely speak the other two just get a fit of the giggles.

'Wha . . . ?' goes Jake. 'Wha? You're not . . . (giggle, giggle) . . . making any . . . (giggle, giggle) . . . sense.'

'Tee-hee-hee!' goes Jools. 'He can't . . . nahahahaha . . . he can't . . . nahahaha . . . speak!'

And these two are snorting and fizzing and going off like two shook-up cans of Coke and laughing at my expense, and I remember feeling pissed off and yet not caring at the same time. I *know* how they got that car pointing forwards up the tunnel, but I just can't explain it, and every time I try the words won't come and my mouth hangs open.

'Look, look, look!' goes Jake, snot running down his nose. 'Look at his . . . (giggle, giggle) face. Look at his little face!'

And they're hooting and howling and Jake's wiping the snot from under his nose and that's about the last thing I remember in the tunnel. Me, overwhelmed by the scent of beautiful Jools, feeling wasted, feeling her shift her weight in my lap as she hugs her ribs and tries to stop herself from laughing. And then the next thing I remember is the thing I can't talk about.

The thing I don't want to remember.

19

Breakfast of Champions

Cookie stands over me at breakfast time, eyeing me as if something might have been mentioned to him about my behaviour during the night, but if so, he says nothing about it. Breakfast is one of his usual 'banquets'. For the veggies, soggy crispies and limp, damp toast. For the tooth-and-claw meat-eaters, sausage and egg. I say 'meat', as if there might actually be some meat inside the two condoms stuffed with lard and low-grade cereal that are leaking hot fat on to my plate. Cookie has managed, with great skill in the kitchen, to burn them black on one side and leave them raw and unpleasantly pink on the other. I wonder where he did his training. I wonder if this is really all a test, to see if we can take it.

'There's another egg if you want one,' says Cookie. To me, apparently. I'm not sure what it is I've done to deserve such mollycoddling. What, another moulded-plastic joke-shop egg? For *me*? Oh, thank you, Cookie! Why, the emperors of ancient Rome never got treated this well.

'I'll pass.'

Cookie looks at Pete, rolls his eyes and goes, 'His lordship says 'e'll pass.'

I've got other things on my mind besides breakfast. Namely, whether anyone noticed my little accident in the night. I think I got away with it, but who knows? I let Interesting Gilbert drift back to sleep before I hurriedly changed my underblankets. I took the damp ones out to the bathroom, washed them, wrung them out and threw them over a radiator.

Okay, it's no big deal. So I pissed in the bed. So what? I'd just rather that Gilb and Amy didn't know. Not to mention Pete. Or Cookie, for Christ's sake. I mean that's *it*, isn't it? If they all think you're a piss-the-bed. Cookie would have gone round behind my back calling me Lord Piss-the-Bed. What can you say for yourself after that? I mean, you wouldn't be allowed an opinion about anything in the world if they knew that. You might suggest that Arsenal are better than Manchester United, and they could say, 'Well, you might think that, but you piss in the bed.' Or you might say, 'Cookie, this toast is a bit black,' only for him to reply, 'Yes, Your Lordship, but you piss in the bed.'

They would just make a big thing out of it. When it isn't a big thing at all.

So I think I got away with it.

Immediately after breakfast is another deeply tiresome yak-yak session with Pete. This is becoming a yawn already. But we're promised, if we're good boys and girls, we will go out caving with Pete later. We muster in the yak-yak room and are each presented with a huge sheet of blank paper from a giant roll plus a bunch of fat, coloured felt-tip pens.

'What I want you to do', says Pete, 'is to draw a road map of your life so far. Like this.'

He then proceeds to scribble pictures along a road, with stick-men and other sketches at important times in his life. He does this pretty quickly, and as he does so he explains what it all means. Pete had a happy childhood but then his mum and dad split up and he and his brothers had to go with his mum to a smaller house and things didn't work out so well. He draws a house torn apart. Later on, further down the road, he draws another house broken apart with zigzag lines and a stick-man crying big fat tears. This is when he got divorced from his wife. As he talks, Amy and I look across at each other: I don't know why.

'That's just an example,' says Pete, 'though you can all probably draw better than me.'

'You're pretty bad,' I say.

'See that man crying?' says Amy. 'Is that really you, or is that just an example?'

'No, that's really me,' answers Pete. 'About five years ago. For about six months after my divorce I couldn't stop crying. It was ridiculous, really. I'd be in the supermarket buying a tin of beans and I'd burst out crying. But that's here, in the past, so I would need to draw more to bring us up to date.'

I can't see the point of this, but both Amy and Gilb seem to go along with it, so I do too. Anything for a quiet life. As for Gilb, he's practically slavering over the felt-tips.

His eyelashes flutter weirdly. I mean, it's his thing, isn't it? He's like a junkie for those pens. He's straight into it.

I give it a go, but there isn't a lot I can put in, so I concentrate on the most recent end of the road map. I make a drawing of the entrance to the Pikehorn Tunnel, with lots of orange flames coming out, when the car caught fire. I look up at the other two. They've both gone quiet, but Gilb is pop-eyed now, dashing colour down like that mad painter who sliced off his own ear: Van Gogh. Amy is quiet, but busy. I don't think there's quite enough stuff in mine, so I go back down my 'road' and put in a picture of Jake first showing me how to break into a car.

Pete sits quietly, watching us. Then he makes a big deal of examining his wristwatch, you know, as if all of a sudden reading the time on a watch is a complicated thing. 'Okay, that will do,' he says. 'Let's talk about what you've done here.'

'I ain't finished,' says Gilb.

'Don't worry about finishing it, Gilbert.'

'I was just getting started,' protests Gilb.

'Look, you're not painting the ceiling of the Sistine Chapel,' says Pete. 'Leave it there and you can do more to it later if you want. The idea is you show the rest of us what you've done and explain it to us. Matt, will you go first?'

'No way am I going first!' I say.

'For God's sake!' says Amy. 'I'll go first if it helps to get us out of here.'

'Good,' says Pete. 'Come and stand over here and hold up your work.'

133

Amy holds up her drawing. I mean her 'work'. It's a lot of stick-men. And smaller stick-figures: children, I suppose. And all of the stick-men are holding . . . well, the stick-men are all holding sticks. And they are hitting the children with the sticks. The children all have speech balloons coming from their mouths but there are no words in the speech balloons. Then, further down the road, the children are lighting fires. To draw her fires, Amy has used the same orange felt-tip as I have.

'Would you talk us through your road map, Amy?' asks Pete.

Amy crosses her legs at her ankles. She on has these neat, dainty elf-boots. She's kind of a pixie, Amy is. 'Well, this is me.' Here she points to all of the little stick-figures. 'This is a man my mum brought into the house. After a short time of living with us he started to hit me. Black and blue. Every day. This is a cupboard where I'd get locked in the dark. He kept me like a dog. Hours at a time, sometimes all night. I know I should have told someone, maybe at school, but you don't, do you? Not when you're just a kid. Here's where I set fire to a rubbish bin at school. It worked, because it got me sent to see a shrink, and the beatings stopped for a little while. But it all started again, and I kept doing it. Though I've stopped now.'

'This is heavy,' says Gilbert. 'Very 'eavy.'

It is heavy. Nothing like that ever happened to me. I might have had a clip round the ear from Dad if he got really mad, but not like this. I'm trying not to stare at Amy. She looks up at me and blinks shyly. Then she sniffs, and wipes her nose quickly with the back of her wrist. 'There's other stuff,' she says, 'worse stuff. But I'm not going there. That's all I'm putting in.'

I realise that Amy has probably done this life-map stuff many times with many different shrinks and counsellors and probation officers. She makes it seem routine. This is her life. Then I come along and without knowing the first thing about her I put her down. I feel bad about that.

'You've been very brave to open up to us, Amy,' says Pete. 'I think we should hear from the other two, and then we'll talk a bit about all the road maps together, okay? Gilbert?'

Amy sits down.

Gilb gets up. 'It ain't finished,' he says again.

'Never mind that.'

Sometimes I think Gilb hasn't spent enough time talking with real people. It's like he does all his talking online. I say this because he's got a sideways smile, like a :-) on a computer. He gives us one of those sideways smiles and unrolls his work for us to see.

I take one look at it and I'm off my chair. 'That is fuckin' brilliant!' I say.

'No swearing, please, Matt. But, yes, it is brilliant.'

We all stand up to look closer, because it is incredibly detailed. The kid has knocked this off in under half an hour, and it's some kind of masterpiece. And the really weird thing is I have no idea what it's supposed to be say-ing. I can see a school gate, I can see dark figures, I can see Gilb in there. But everything twists into something else, like in a dream where the edge of one thing becomes another thing.

Factoid number sixty-eight: a kid may look like a dork but he might be a genius. 'Brilliant,' I hear myself repeating.

'And that's a real compliment, coming from him,' says Amy, jerking a thumb in my direction.

For some reason, I take big exception to this. 'What do you mean by that?'

'Well, you never usually have anything good to say about anyone.'

I feel my cheeks burning. What happened? I give the dork a round of applause and she uses it to take a pop at me. I'm just about to say something nasty back at her when Pete stops me. 'I think Amy was paying you a compliment, Matt. Amy, would you like to say what you meant, but find a better way of putting it?'

'Dunno what the fuss is about,' says Amy. 'I'm just saying I like you better when you're positive instead of slagging off everything.'

'Yeh,' snorts Gilbert. 'Me too.'

'Me too,' says Pete, 'and I expect Gilbert was pretty pleased at the way you reacted to his drawing.'

I look at Gilb and he blinks back at me. I still feel like I'm being attacked. I thought this was supposed to be about Gilb, not about me, and I say so.

'It's about all of us,' says Pete. 'About how we are treated. And about how we treat each other. So let's talk about Gilbert's drawing.'

20

Flaming the Flamers

After Gilb, it's my turn. To show my road map, I mean. It looks a bit cruddy compared to Gilb's awesome work of art, but I hold it up in the air and tell them what there is to tell. Amy stretches out on the floor, belly-down, propping her chin up with her hands. Her eyes have narrowed, and she's way too over-focused on me. It makes me nervous.

Anyway, I show them the point on the road where Jake first taught me how to take a car and how easy it was, and how we got into it big time. Then I jump to the tunnel, which is where my life kind of ends. There is my crap drawing of the Testarossa. Well, it looks kind of like a Jag, but it doesn't matter, because it's on fire.

'That's it, really,' I say. 'My wonderful life.'

If I'm expecting sympathy here, which I am, I don't get it.

'You've drawn three people in the burning car,' says Amy. 'Who's the third one?'

I take a deep breath. 'That's Jools. The one I told you about. She got pretty badly scarred.'

'Yeh, but who is she?' Gilb wants to know.

'She is . . . *was* Jake's girlfriend.'

Pete looks at me strangely. He shapes his mouth to say something, then he stops himself.

There's an uncomfortable silence so I find myself talking just to fill in the gap. 'I mean, it was Jake's fault. He was to blame, not me. About Jools, I mean. About all of it.'

I know I'm just burbling, but I don't know what they want me to say. Pete's rubbing his chin and still looking at me kind of strangely. Gilb, as usual, looks like he's trying to remember his own name. And Amy has her hand up in the air, which is ridiculous because we're not in school and there are only four of us in the room, but she has her hand up as if waiting for me or Pete or whoever to give her permission to speak.

'Go ahead, Amy,' says Pete.

'I'm not being funny,' she says, which is what people say when they're going to be difficult, 'but you did it differently to how me and Gilb did it.'

'Did what?'

'Did our road maps. Yours is different.'

'Yeh, well, you didn't flame a car, that's why.'

'No,' says Amy, shaking her head. 'That's not what I mean. I don't mean about what happened, that I got beaten, Gilb was a loner, you flamed a car, du-du-du.'

She actually says, 'du-du-du'. I think she means 'dot-dot-dot', but I don't tell her.

'Go on, Amy,' says Pete.

Amy twists her mouth a bit before speaking. 'Well, I said how much I felt hurt and betrayed. Gilb said how

138

lonely he felt as an outsider and he started doing his paintings to escape. Even Pete told us he was bawling his eyes out in the supermarket.'

'"Even Pete". Thanks, Amy,' says Pete, but he's smiling.

'I don't mean anything,' says Amy to reassure Pete. She turns back to me. 'But with your road map you only tell us what happened. Not how it felt.'

This bugs me again for some reason. I feel myself going red from the neck up, but I manage to keep a smile on my face. 'And your point is?'

'Just that. You give us the cold facts but you ain't said how it felt. How you felt about the whole thing.'

'How it felt? It felt hot. You know what hot is, don't you? You'd know all about that, wouldn't you, Miss Creepy Fire-bug?'

'I suppose I do.'

'So?'

'So it says stuff about your personality. You're holding something back. Maybe from yourself.'

'OOOOOOOOOOOOOOOOOOOH,' I go, way too loud. 'Listen to Dolly Shrink! Hark at the junior psychologist!'

'Matt,' goes Pete.

'And where's your diploma, Miss Fuckin' Hair-scare? Who are you to look inside someone else's head –'

'Matt, calm down.'

'– when your own head is a bird's nest of evil nightmares and dripping blood and torn feathers and and and and and –'

'Matt! STOP THIS NOW!' Pete is up on his feet.

He takes my road map out of my hand, shoves my arm up my back and hustles me out of the room. I see the bastard wink – yes, he winks! – at the other two and he says, 'Take a break.'

Pete leads me outside into the yard and he tries to sit me down on the low wall by the car park, but I'm trembling and so supercharged with anger that I could easily walk up the side of a mountain. Pete sits down himself and watches me wringing my hands. Then he takes out an old-fart's oily tin of tobacco, opens it and proceeds to roll himself a pathetically thin cigarette.

'Very calming, rolling a cigarette,' he says. He's very precise in the way he crumbles the tobacco, rolls it in a paper, licks the gummed edge and sticks it down. 'Want one?'

I accept it. He lights me.

After a couple of puffs of this feeble straw I take my place on the wall beside him.

'Wow,' says Pete, 'I've heard about this anger.'

'Yeh, you probably have it on file somewhere.'

'Probably. Do you feel better? Take a deep breath.'

'I don't need a deep breath.'

'Take one anyway.'

I do one for him, big breath and big sigh on the exhale, all theatre, of course, but sometimes you've got to give these people what they want.

'Good. Feel better?'

'Yes.'

'Ready to go back in there and fix things?'

I know perfectly well what's coming. 'I'm prepared to accept an apology from Amy, yes.'

'Ha!' goes Pete, and he actually slaps his thigh. 'Ha! Let's have a rethink on that, shall we?'

I can't be bothered. I just ... Can't. Be. Bothered. We could have an hour of back and forth and who said what and who insulted whom and at the end of it all he'd still want me to apologise to Lady Death-head in there.

'Okay,' I say, standing up. 'I'll apologise.'

I throw away what's left of the skinny ciggy and march back through the doors. He has to chuck away his own half-smoked roll-up to follow me inside. Amy and Gilb are pretty much where we left them. They look up as I crash open the door.

I storm over to Amy and stand over her. She's still lying on the floor, but is now on her side. She looks up at me. There's something in her eye. It's not fear. It's almost a challenge, as if to say: 'Go on, kick me, I've had a lot worse than that before breakfast.' Pete is right behind me.

'Amy, I'd like to apologise, for saying anything. I have a temper problem but I'm trying to control it. I didn't mean to go at you like that. I hope you'll accept my apology.'

She looks surprised. She looks at Gilb, but he's staring at the pattern in the carpet as usual. His face hangs, like a frozen computer. Anyway, she goes, 'Yeh.'

I look at Pete, as if to say: 'That satisfy you?' Then I sit down.

'Right,' says Pete. 'Let's all sit down and talk some more about our road maps.'

21

The Original Everything-Happens-to-Me Kid

Following the yak-yak, flame, road-map, tyre-track, burn-out, whatever session, we get to go caving, or pot-holing. Sometimes Pete calls it pot-holing and sometimes he calls it caving, and when I seriously – and I mean seriously – ask him what's the difference, he just says, 'Give it a rest, Matt.'

I hate that. When you're being deadly serious or completely straight and somebody thinks you're taking the piss.

Anyway, we get driven deeper into the Peak District and down into the dales. The weather has come over cloudy and there's a whiff of rain in the air. Pete warns us that if it does rain, the water goes straight down the sink holes and we might get a bit wet. Gilb and Amy seem up for it, but crawling around in a wet underground passage is not my idea of fun. However, it's better than yet another session of meaningless soul-raking yak-yak.

I see another minibus, a red one, parked up ahead of us, on a deserted country road. Pete comes to a stop right behind it. The driver of the other bus is sitting reading a newspaper. Pete will not be joining us while we're squirming about in caves. Instead, we're to be guided by Alex, Sarah's boyfriend.

If you ask me, Alex looks like a stoner. His eyes are bloodshot, either from lack of sleep or from his cave-dwelling lifestyle. That's it: he's either doing the dope or he spends most of his life in darkness down a pot-hole. He's a tall, lanky streak of a man with his hair tied back in a pony-tail, and I think: For God's sake, Sarah, a pony-tail? Is this the best you can do? Surely a good-looking woman like you doesn't have to settle for a guy with a pony-tail. I think I might mention this to her when I get back.

We pile out of the minibus.

'Why, what a rabble,' says Alex. He says it with a smile, but I know he means it. Then he opens the rear doors of his red minibus and begins dragging out equipment. Overalls. Helmets. Lamps. Boots of all sizes. Nylon and steel rope-ladders. Serious gear. 'Get kitted-up,' he says. 'We want to be in and *oot* before the *rairn* comes.' He's got one of those slow, lazy Geordie accents, like someone just got him out of bed with a hangover. In the *rairn*.

I hear Pete and Alex discussing the rain. Alex looks at the sky. He seems a bit doubtful about the whole expedition. Alex says they've had a lot of rain lately and the water-table is unusually high. I also hear him ask, in a low voice, if we're all sensible. Pete, by way of an answer, the bastard, just gives a twitch of his nose.

We pull on nylon overalls and each put on a helmet. It's a bit of a giggle. We all look like coal-miners with a helmet lamp and a battery pack, and I make Amy and Gilb laugh by going, 'Aye lad, where's thy ferret' and other coal-miner-type things.

'Give over,' says Alex, spoiling the fun. 'You need to listen to a few things. First, this is going to have to be a short trip *doon*, 'cos I'm keeping an eye on the weather. Second, this is an exercise in trust. If we can't trust each other, we can get lost or hurt. I'm taking three of you down there and I want to bring three of you back, so keep your ears and your eyes open. You look out for each other, is that clear?'

Yep, we got it. Yep, yep, yep. Stop talking, let's go.

And three-quarters of an hour later we're in a cavern thirty feet below the surface and my foot is stuck.

'If you're pissing about,' says Alex, his face three inches from mine and his lamp shining in my eyes, 'I'll be really annoyed.'

'I am NOT pissing about! My foot is completely STUCK.'

I really am not messing. What's happened is we've gone through a crawl-hole in the dark. This is after walking through dark passages head high, shoulder high, waist high and then wading through water up to our shins. Alex has promised us that if we wriggle through this crawl-hole on our bellies we come out into what he told us was an amazing limestone cavern with a small underwater lake. But I can't move.

'Has this happened before?' I say.

I see him blink. 'Never. And I've taken over two hundred kids through this tunnel.'

Amy is behind me in the tunnel, her way forward blocked by me, and she's asking what's going on. I tell her I'm stuck, and I hear her relaying the information to Gilb, who brings up the rear because Alex decided he was the most sensible. The crawl-hole is only about eighteen inches high. I'm flat out on my belly. We're all wearing these heavy industrial boots and somehow as I crawled through my right boot got jammed, toe and heel, at the side of the tunnel where the roof almost meets the floor, at a place where I'd tried to kick myself through. It's like the rock is a set of jaws clamped around my boot.

'Can you go backwards?' says Alex.

I've tried already, but I try again. No good. My foot won't budge.

'Try flexing your foot.'

It's all no good. Amy shuffles back and Gilb squeezes past her and has a go at kicking my foot free. Useless. Even Alex tries, by grabbing the collar of my overalls, to drag me through, but I don't move an inch. After several minutes of trying various different things, I see, caught in the light from my lamp, a big bead of sweat run all the way down Alex's face. For the first time I realise he's worried.

Somehow he sees my thoughts. 'Don't panic,' he says. 'Look, can you call back to Amy?'

'Amy!'

'Yeh! What's happening?'

Amy can't hear Alex but she can hear me, so I have to relay everything Alex says. He tells me to ask her if she can reach my boot.

'Can you reach my boot?'

'Only just. Yes, but only just.'

'Tell her', goes Alex, 'to see if she can untie your bootlace.'

'Amy, untie my bootlace!' I can feel her scrabbling around my foot. 'Can you reach?'

'I can just get my fingers round. I'm trying to untie the lace. I can't really get my fingers in far enough.'

'Tell her to keep trying.'

'Amy, keep trying!'

Then Amy goes, 'Oh, shit.'

'What is it?'

'The lace has pulled into a tight knot. And there's another thing.'

'What is it?'

'Gilb says that water is running into the tunnel. It must be raining outside.'

'What is it?' asks Alex.

I tell him. Just his face is illuminated by my own lamp, a few inches away from me. He closes his eyes. He blows out his cheeks really slowly. Another bead of sweat runs down from under his helmet.

He opens his eyes again. 'Matt, this is what I'm going to do. I'm going to leave you for a few minutes. I can get out of the cave up ahead through another hole. Then I'll run back to where we came in and come up behind you. Then I'll have you out.'

'You sure of that?'

'I'm sure. Keep talking to Amy. I'll be about half an hour. You okay with that?'

'What about the water? Amy just told me it's really started to pour in.'

'I'll be half an hour at most.'

That hasn't answered the question about the water. Anyway, I tell him I'm okay, and he's gone. By now I'm shivering, even though I don't feel particularly cold. I can actually feel the water trickling underneath my belly. I wonder exactly how long it will take before the tunnel is completely submerged. I wonder if it's more or less than half an hour. I explain to Amy what's going on. Something touches my skin near the top of my boot. 'What's that?'

'It's my finger,' says Amy.

'What are you doing?'

'Nothing. I'll leave my finger there so you know I'm here.'

'Thanks, Amy.' I really mean thanks, too, but somehow it comes out like *thanks a bunch*.

Then Amy tells me when she was locked in the dark cupboard she used to pat her knee and pretend it was someone else looking out for her. We talk for a while, and the talking helps me pretend I'm not scared. I can hear Gilb murmuring behind her, suggesting things she might say to me.

Even while we're talking my mind is running through other things. I wonder why this has happened to me. I know I might die if the tunnel fills up with water before they get me out. I'm the original every-thing-happens-to-me kid.

When I was a little kid I was the one who got his head stuck in the railings of the school fence. Jake had to get me out. A few years later one winter I fell through the ice on the local pond. Luckily, Jake was there to pull me out. Notice how it wasn't Jake who these things happened to. No, it was always me. Alex said he has brought two hundred kids through this tunnel, with never a problem until I come along. I think my card must be marked.

I have no way of knowing how long Alex has been gone. It's hard keeping the talk going but when it stops it is good to feel Amy's finger on my leg. My eyes feel tired, so I let them close. Then I hear something up ahead, in front of me: footsteps coming through the cavern. My first thought is that Alex has failed to get out up ahead, and that he's had to come back.

There is a light, but it isn't a torch-beam. It's a tiny, flickering flame, dancing ahead of me. I feel a wave of cold and I shiver again. The tiny flame floats in the air and then comes closer. At last I see a face under the flame, pale and yellow. The flame is a candle and it is wedged into the front of an old-fashioned miner's helmet. I know the face underneath the helmet.

'What's tha doin' there, lad?'

It's Jake.

I blink. I know I'm not dreaming, because I can feel Amy rubbing her finger on my leg. 'Jake,' I whisper. 'Am I going to die?'

He has a pickaxe and a lighted brass Davy lamp. He's wearing a pit vest and his face is smeared with black coal dust: a proper miner. The whites of his eyes and his white teeth shine through the black dust on his face. 'Is tha goin' to die? Tha bloody well should!'

'Jake!' The rubbing around my foot increases.

'Why won't tha just tell 'em? Eh, lad? Why won't tha? 'Cos you're a twat, that's why! Why won't tha just tell 'em the bloody truth!'

'Jake! Amy, help me! It's Jake!' I don't know if Amy hears me. But something is squeezing my boot, gnawing at it. It's like a dog has got hold of it in its jaw.

'I'm sick o' thee, Matt! Sick o' thee! I'm sick o' bein' called here over and over. I ought to tek this 'ere pickaxe and run it through your eye, you lying little twat! Why can't you speak the truth for once in your useless life?'

He's spitting mad. Then he raises his pickaxe as if to strike me in the face. I scream at him to stop. Then I'm screaming and screaming all over again, until through my own screaming I hear Amy shouting at me.

'Matt! Matt! I've cut your bootlace. See if you can pull your foot out of the boot.'

I drag my leg hard and my ankle works itself half free. Another kick gets my foot out of the stuck boot and I can scramble forward, free of the crawl-hole and into the higher chamber. I stand there breathing heavily, shivering and panting, and I look around and Jake has gone. I want to shout to tell Amy that I've kicked free but I can't get out any words.

I stand there, breathing the damp, salty air of that limestone cavern, the light from my helmet lamp playing on the streaked walls. I'm in a cavern with a tiny lake, and with stalactites hanging from the cave roof and stalagmites all round me. I hear a movement in the crawl-hole and I see Amy wriggling into the chamber. She's all smiles and I think I'M IN LOVE WITH AMY, so I hug her so tight and she hugs me back and I'm going, 'Oh oh oh oh oh oh oh oh.'

'I remembered my little penknife,' she says. 'I sawed off your bootlace.'

But I don't care about all that. I just want to keep hugging her. It turns out that Alex hasn't even returned yet, and that Amy sorted the problem by herself. She breaks off from me and suggests we go back to Gilb, who is waiting on the other side of the crawl-hole. I'm a bit freaked about the idea of getting in there again, but Amy points out that if I take off my other boot there will be no danger of getting stuck a second time. The fact is, I'm so keen to get to the upper ground and put all this caving behind me that I do what she says and I slide through the crawl-hole, this time like a little weasel, with no problem at all.

Gilb is on the other side with his mouth hanging half open and I think I'm in love with him, too, because I give him a huge hug. Just as I have Gilb in a clinch Alex appears.

He's carrying new equipment. He doesn't look too pleased. 'Have you been messing me about, you little bastard?'

All my joy, my ecstasy, is punctured right there. 'No!' That's all I can think to say.

Alex doesn't look convinced. Amy shows him her penknife and explains how her quick thinking has sprung me. Alex dips his head to direct his torch-beam at my feet. He sees my sodden socks. 'Come on. Let's get out of here.'

22

It's All Smiles at the Arnedale Lodge

Alex has to trail us back to Arnedale Lodge to write up an incident report. There you are: I'm an 'incident' now. It's official. An incident waiting to happen.

Of course, by the time we get back to the bus and Alex has told Pete about what happened they both seem to find it amusing. Frankly, if you take a kid down a pot-hole and get him stuck and risk his life as the cave starts to fill up with torrential rain, then I don't see that as a laughing matter. I don't see what's so hilarious about a kid drowned by the probation service.

They're still joking about it when we get back. They tell Cookie there was nearly one less for tea, and he quips that it would have made his job easier. Arf arf arf! Well, slap my thigh! Oh, my ribs, I shall expire from laughing! One less sausage to blacken. One less egg to char to a crisp. Fifteen fewer lardy chips for the fat bastard to count out.

Plus, I think Alex owes me an apology for accusing me of messing around. He comes in with Pete, both jangling their minibus keys as if the pair of them think they've accomplished a good day's work. I suggest the apology to him.

The pair of them hang up their jackets on the coat-rack by reception and I see Pete slip his minibus keys in his jacket pocket while he watches how Alex is going to answer me. 'Well,' Alex goes in that lazy way of his, 'you could be right. But from what I hear, you're such a stranger to the truth you can't blame me for thinking you were just winding me up, like.'

'What does that mean?'

Alex looks at Pete. Amy and Gilb have appeared, too, and they're listening. 'What I say. Stranger to the truth. A teller of porkie pies.'

'Who, me?' I say. 'You talking about me?'

Alex laughs this off. 'Come on, let's eat.'

'No,' I say, and I can feel my cheeks burning. 'I want to know what you mean.'

Alex sniffs and looks me dead in the eye. 'Well, from what Sarah tells me, you've got a very inventive imagination.'

'Yeh? Well, Sarah's got hairy legs,' I hear myself say, incredibly.

'What?'

Pete steps between us. 'No, Alex just doesn't want to say it. But he's talking about Jake. Yes?'

I'm dumbfounded by this. Lost for words.

Then Pete says, 'Come on, let's see what there is in the trough.'

They all turn away and go through to the canteen. But I'm stunned. I have no answer. After a while I follow them in. I don't eat much. I have no appetite. I have no energy. I'm like a ghost. I see Amy eyeing me strangely.

Another yak-yak session takes place after dinner. I don't say much. Pete wants to know how I felt about getting stuck. It's pretty obvious what I felt. And what I felt about Amy literally getting me out of the hole. Pete probes, but I just don't feel like talking. Though I must say that Amy was a star, and Gilb also did everything he could.

I think a lot about that: about being stuck in a dark place, and about who you can count on when the chips are down. About how someone might stick with you, or show you a light, or extend their finger in the dark. I want to say that. More to Amy and Gilb than to Pete. It seems important. But I don't want to give Pete the pleasure of filling his stupid yak-yak sessions. I just don't feel like talking.

Finally, as if to provoke me, Pete says, 'Well, it seems to me that you were more upset by what Alex said than you were about getting trapped.'

I turn my stare on him. My poison-tipped, acid-dipped, dart-eyed stare.

'You might as well face up to it one day, Matt.' Yes, Pete is deliberately goading me now. The others don't know it, but he is.

'Face up to what?' says Amy.

Gilb looks up at me through his spiked fringe.

Pete stands up and grabs my road map, which is still in the room from the previous session. He unrolls it and points to the naff picture of Jake. 'Who is this,

Matt? Who is this figure? I mean who *exactly*?'

'That's his brother Jake,' says Gilb, surprising me by coming to my aid.

But Pete holds up a single finger to stop Gilb from saying any more. 'No. I want Matt to tell us.'

I'm looking out of the window. Jake has appeared on the other side of the glass, still in his pit helmet, his pickaxe slung across his shoulder, mocking me. He's scratching at the window, grinning.

'Come on, Matt,' goads Pete. 'Isn't it time you admitted one or two things to yourself? Isn't it time you came clean about *Jake*?'

Again I don't answer.

Amy pipes up with, 'I don't think that's fair! I don't think that's fair to get him to talk about his brother after what happened. There are things people just can't talk about, even to friends.'

'Thank you, Amy,' says Pete firmly. Now he has a lop-sided smile on his face, like a skid-mark on a pair of underpants. 'But I'm not your friend. I'm your proba-tion officer. All three of you are here for things you've done, and for which I'm holding you responsible. What's more, I'll be the one who decides what is fair and what isn't fair.'

Amy is stung. She winds her neck back in.

'Jake wasn't there, was he, Matt?' says Pete.

Amy and Gilb turn their attention towards me.

'He wasn't there that night. He *couldn't* have been there, could he, Matt?'

'No,' I say. It comes out in a whisper.

'What's that?'

'No,' I say again.

Now Amy and Gilb are looking straight at me, puzzled. As if they can't understand any of it.

'Do you want to explain why?' says Pete.

'No.'

'But Jake's been unfairly getting the blame for quite a few things, hasn't he, Matt?'

I don't answer this. I'm watching Jake at the window, who by now is making all sorts of mocking faces, leering, jeering, cheering, giving me the finger, enjoying my discomfort.

Pete stares at me in silence for a long time. Amy hugs herself, as if a sudden breeze has come through the window to make her feel cold.

Finally, Pete sighs and looks at his watch. 'All right, let's call that a starting point. We can get into it again tomorrow morning, and maybe we can settle the question of Jake once and for all.'

The session breaks up and Gilb follows me back to our room. He says nothing. It's weird. We both lie down on our bunks. After a while Pete comes in. 'Matt, you all right?' he says.

I sit up and flash him a smile to show that none of it has touched me. 'Yeh, I'm all right.'

'You are here to be pushed. You know that, don't you?'

'I know that.' I flash him another smile. 'I'm all right, Pete.'

'Okay. If you want to talk to me in private, you know where I am.'

'Thanks, Pete.'

He backs out of the door. I'm still smiling at the space he occupied before he left, but I'm feeling like a caged animal. Trapped. Two minutes later there's a little knock on the door. I don't answer, so after a while Gilb says, 'Come in.'

It's Amy. Gilb sits up. I don't. She leans against the wall. She's still sort of hugging herself. Eventually she says to Gilb, 'He's going to make a break for it.'

'What?' says Gilb.

'You are, aren't you, Matt? I'm right. I know I am.'

I don't answer.

'I've been in enough care homes to see it coming. I always knew when one of the kids was going to make a break. They go meek. They smile a lot. You know: co-operate. The ones who are screaming and shouting don't run.'

I say nothing. But she's right.

'So can I come with you?'

'Me too,' says Gilb.

'What?' I sit up. I'm amazed. 'Why the hell would you want to come with me? You both look like you're having a good time here.'

'A good time?' says Amy. 'Are you insane? This place is doing my head in.'

'Yeh, all the talking,' says Gilb. 'I mean, fuck this set-up.'

'So, you're just going along with things, huh?'

Amy and Gilb look at each other, as if I'm the slow one.

I get off the bunk and start packing things into my bag. 'You don't want to come with me. There are things about me you don't know and if you did, you wouldn't want to come with me.'

'What things?' asks Amy.

Still stuffing socks and pants into my bag, I say, 'Factoid number one: I piss the bed –'

'I knew that,' says Gilb.

'Factoid number two: I am a pathological liar, apparently.'

'What's pathological?' Amy asks me.

I realise I don't know what it means. I probably go around using hundreds of words and I don't really know what they mean. 'A compulsive liar. Can't help myself.'

'So am I,' says Amy.

'And me,' says Gilb.

'Everyone lies,' Amy says. 'Teachers who pretend they like you. Probation officers who say they care but who'd rather see you banged up. Politicians who want your vote. Businessmen who want your money. Magistrates and police who want to wipe the floor with you. Boys who want to screw you. Parents who would rather see you dead –'

'Stop, Amy.' I don't like where she's going with this. 'My parents don't want to see me dead.'

'Well, I'm just saying everyone lies.'

I stop packing to look at them. The three of us make a really pretty A-team, don't we? 'I'm talking about huge lies. Fantastic lies. Lies as big as a space station. Bigger.'

I know it doesn't matter what I say. Somehow they know they're coming with me. I haven't said they can: they just know it.

'How are we going to do it?' asks Amy.

'Pack your bag and be ready. Go to bed. Heads down. All normal.'

Amy makes to leave, but then she turns. 'If you two go without me, I'll track you down and burn you.'

I look her deep in the eye. She means it.

23

Counting Backwards Will Make You King

It's nearly one o'clock in the morning. I tap on Amy's door and she opens it immediately, as if she's been standing there all night with her fingers on the handle. 'Bags packed?' I ask her.

'Yeh.'

'Go into the canteen,' I say.

'What?'

'You see where Cookie keeps those big pots of marmalade?'

'Aren't they locked up?'

'No, the jam pots and the marmalade are left out. Bring me one of those great big pots. Full.'

'Why?'

'You want to come with me or not?'

She makes to go to the canteen. I stop her and ask for her penknife, the one she used to cut my bootlaces in the cave. She blinks and reaches down inside her knickers, withdrawing the penknife. Then off she goes to the kitchen.

I go back in the room. Gilb is there with a bedsheet

spread out on the floor like I told him. I give him the penknife. 'Cut the sheet to almost exactly the size of the window,' I say. He doesn't question me; he just goes straight to it.

While Gilb is doing that I go and fetch Amy's bag. We're all packed and ready to leave. The place is quiet. I need to get us out without waking anyone. The doors are all dead-bolt locked and the windows have security bolts on them to stop them from being opened more than an inch.

Amy comes back with this huge caterer's size pot of strawberry jam. 'All quiet out there, Amy?'

'Yeh. What's this for? You hungry?'

Gilb has finished cutting the sheet to size. 'Empty it on that sheet?'

'What?'

'Are you going to question everything I say? Just empty it and smear it all over the sheet.'

Amy twists the cap off the jam pot and dumps the strawberry jam on the sheet. She looks at me and I nod. Then she smears the jam all round the sheet. She giggles. Gilb helps her. I encourage them to get it into the corners and all over. When it's done I pick up the sheet and take it over to the window. I press it to the glass and the jam makes it stick well.

Then I ball up one of the blankets from my bunk. I tell the other two to wipe their hands on the sheet off-cut, because we're ready to go. I push the balled-up blanket against the window. It's toughened security glass and it won't give way easily. I have to get Gilb to hold the balled-up blanket against the glass. I swing up on to his bunk and I kick hard with the heel of my boot. The glass breaks with a soft pop, like a cork coming out of a bottle. The splinters of glass stick to the sheet and make barely a sound. I tap out the shards at the edge of the window and most of the glass comes out in one piece on the sheet, which I then lower to the ground outside.

We're out. I go first, Amy comes second and Gilb hands the bags through the window before climbing out himself. There's a three-quarter moon shining down on us, more light than we would like, but no one seems to have heard a thing. The night air is crisp and cold. So far, so good.

'What now?' whispers Amy.

'I'm getting the minibus.'

'They'll hear you start it up!'

'I'm going to roll it all the way down the slope before I turn over the engine. You wait here and you'll see me come by with the bus.'

There's a security light I can't help tripping, but I've noticed it come on in the night myself while I was lying awake, maybe if a fox or a cat comes by. I scramble across the lawn in the full glare of the security light. I don't hesitate in getting the minibus door open before climbing into the driver's seat. All I have to do is take off the handbrake and the minibus rolls down the driveway. I stop it by the gate and Amy and Gilb come pelting across the lawn. They climb in beside me.

'Christ,' says Gilb. 'How did you do it so fast?'

'There's an easy way to get into cars and a *very* easy way,' I say, holding up the bunch of keys I took from Pete's pocket.

All the way home in that minibus? You must be joking: Not on your nelly, as my dad would say. First, it's a marker. I don't expect that anyone at the lodge heard us leave, but it's always possible, and if they did they would immediately get the police to put out a call. Second, if I'm going to take a motor and get nicked for it, which of course is inevitable, I might as well be hung for a sheep as a lamb: so I'll be driving home something other than an engine that's seen more farts than a weightlifter's shorts.

At the outskirts of a town called Ashbourne we donate the scrap-metal of the minibus to God by parking it outside a small church so that we can go looking for some real tin. Something with at least *some* grunt.

'What about one of those,' goes Gilb, spying a Lexus conveniently parked in the shadows.

'Certainly, Gilb, if that's what you want. Meet Stuart.'

'Ooo's Stuart?' goes Gilb.

I set down my backpack. The seams are held together by Velcro, so I can easily open them and get to the metal frame. The frame itself pops apart, and two sections of it, when dismantled and pushed together again, make my Slim Jim, my Stuart. What? Did you think I would go anywhere without my best friend? They think they are so clever, emptying our bags. But I'm equipped. Ready for business. And I love an audience.

As it happens, with Amy watching me and Gilb timing me, I make a muff of disabling the alarm on the Lexus. It goes off for maybe six or seven seconds before I can damp it. We all duck back into the shadows, but no one comes out. My overall time for getting the Lexus running, not counting hiding in the shadows, is sixty-nine seconds: not bad, but not my personal best.

Jake used to like a Lexus. He could have had it rolling inside half a minute.

'And is the Lexus somewhat more comfortable for you, Madam Amy?' I ask once we're under way.

'Yes, much more,' says Amy.

'And for you, jolly Sir Gilb?'

'Much better, Your Lordship,' says Gilb.

There's even a road map on the back seat and a packet of Mint Imperials in the glove compartment. We take the back roads, hoping to keep away from police patrols. We're high on escape fumes and cold, graveyard-shift night air.

I stop the Lexus in some turnip-town called Kirby Muxloe. No, I'm not making it up. It's a real place.

'What's up?' Amy wants to know.

'I think Your Ladyship would be more comfortable in an Audi. What does Sir Gilb, Minister for Midnight Paintings, think of that?'

'Oh, jolly, jolly good,' says Sir Gilb.

The thing is, I've clocked the Audi parked in a monster driveway. It's a good idea to keep switching cars. I do a wipe-down in case of fingerprints – I *always* wipe down; Jake used to insist on it – and we leave the Lexus in the street but take the road map and the packet of Mint Imperials. That now makes us thieves rather than twocers, if you're counting the credits, but we need the map to negotiate the back roads. Okay, I'll take the rap for the mints.

About forty seconds. Alarm goes 'wop-wop' and then it's off, but we dive back under the trees all the same. No lights come on in the house. 'Patience, Your Grace,' I counsel Amy as we breathe heavily under the leaves by the gravelled driveway. 'Patience.' I must admit I'm enjoying myself. I'm doing what I do best.

We're in, we're gone. And my guests in this movie like the Audi very much, thank you. It's a smart car. Full spec. On the dash there is even a route planner to help me avoid all the major intersections and floodlit, camera-plagued motorways. There is a speed-camera alert, there's a . . . Oh dear.

'Enjoy it while you can. We'll have to change again in, say, half an hour or so.'

'Isn't it risky to keep switching?' says Gilb.

'I think this one has got a tracking device. Just in case the owners do miss it. Or maybe it is night-time sensitive: if the owner never takes it out at night, it might already be transmitting.'

'What?' Amy looks worried.

'Never fear,' I tell her. 'The technology is out of this world, but Plod is a century behind. Even if they do tune in, we've got a bit of time yet. Have another Mint Imperial.'

We dump the Audi in Market Harborough. No particular reason for the choice of town. I'm just collecting fucked-up place names as we cut across country. Anyway, we cruise around looking for a good swap – I do not intend to make it home in a Skoda or a Ford Ka or anything daft. In the end I have to drive right into town. We park up, get out, wipe down and in the street round the corner from a night club I walk smack into a TVR Cerbera and I go, 'Tee-hee-hee!'

Grunt! This is grunt! It should have 'GRUNT' painted on its sides.

Do you believe in destiny? Do you believe it's all planned out ahead of you and you can't change a single thing? I see that cherry-red, fire-spitting V8 and I just *know* that it was put there for me, right here, right now.

'It's only got two seats,' says Amy.

'You'll have to sit on Gilb's lap,' I tell her. 'Go to the top of the street and keep an eye out. I haven't done one of these before.'

Which is true. Jake had never done one, either. Ever. And it takes me almost five minutes. *Five minutes!* That's a downright embarrassment. Pants. A kind of personal disgrace. But I know it's all part of the script. It's kind of a test. If the doors had been open and the key hanging in the ignition, it wouldn't have been right. The alarm takes a few moments to dampen but in the town no one gives a toss about alarms. It's when alarms *stop* going off that you feel spooked.

But the Cerbera!

It growls. It barks when you tickle the gas. Amy and

Gilb get in and buckle up, but I'm not racing anywhere. I'm saving this. They don't understand what we've got here. No one does. Up to 60 m.p.h. in four seconds. Could rocket to 200. Yes! Up to speeds of 150 m.p.h. this thing can out-accelerate a Tornado jet! When I say it spits fire, I mean it. It has valve overlap that pumps so much fuel into the chamber the surplus sprays into the exhaust and ignites there. Flames everyone can see. This car is on fucking fire! This is a hell car! Hear that grunt? That is the grunt of demon force.

'Calm down!' says Amy as I tell them all this shit.

'Petrol head,' says Gilb.

Petrol head. As if it's an insult. I am most certainly one of those. And I'm sitting in petrol-head nirvana, driving sweetly and sedately out of Market Whatwasit, and I'm still talking, telling a solvent-sniffer and a fire-starter, two people who don't know and don't care, the truly stunning specification of this awesome set of wheels. They don't care, but they are high just by breathing my high.

Although after another thirty or forty miles of driving, even the elation of having dropped on this Cerbera begins to flag, just a little. Amy and Gilb have gone quiet. I know what they're thinking. They're thinking about the music. As in the music that has to be faced. There is the high when you do something reckless and the come-down when you know you're going to be faced with the mess.

But I don't even want to think about that. We're almost home and I'm probably the only one of us with a plan. To take my mind off the music, I silently practise the count, looking for the sequence. There's not much traffic on the back roads at about three in the morning, but even so it starts to happen. There's a light mist rolling in the fields, a will o' the wisp. It just adds to the eeriness of what passes.

There's a Saab 9-3, which I've never done in less than three minutes. Then a Vauxhall Corsa skims by, which is two ten. This is followed by a Toyota Corolla (sixty three seconds). Shortly after, a Ford Ka (forty-three seconds). Bloody hell, a BMW 320Ci (thirty-five seconds). It's happening, but in reverse. My best times, all aligned, but going backwards. Then, stone me, a Peugeot 206 comes along (twenty-nine seconds).

I run through the list again, recapping on what I've just seen, checking for a mistake. I can hardly believe it: 180, 130, 63, 43, 35, 29. It's for real. This is it.

'What are you counting?' Amy blinks at me sleepily.

'Time is running backwards,' I say.

'What are you taking about?'

'This is it,' I tell her, turning off the road.

Gilb wakes up. 'We're going into a field?' he says.

'Do you believe in destiny?' I ask them both. We bump across the grass and then we glide into the entrance to the tunnel. I stop the car, kill the lights and leave the engine bubbling quietly.

'Where are we? What's this place?' says Amy.

'This', I tell them, 'is the Pikehorn Tunnel.'

Gilb scratches his head. 'Yeh. I know this place. This is a bad gaff.'

I tell Amy and Gilb that they have to go, that I need to be on my own to accomplish what needs to be done. I apologise for not dropping them at their houses. They have to understand I don't want to be cruising around in a red Cerbera at this time of the morning. They will have to walk through town to get home.

'What needs to be done?' says Amy.

'Yeh,' goes Gilb. 'What are you on about? And why do we have to go?'

So I tell them. Right there, I decide to tell them the whole thing.

24

The Truth Will Set You Free

About what really happened that night.

Jake was nowhere near. How could he be? The part about Jools was true, though, unfortunately. She was with me. The thing about it being her birthday was true, too. How she looked gorgeous on her birthday night, the way she smelled so wonderful, the perfect, breathless appearance of her; all of that. That was all so true it would burn a hole in your heart.

The only thing different was that Jake wasn't there with us. My brother Jake, you see, was already dead at the time.

Jake had died in a car smash – a completely different car smash – two years before. Jake, who had taught me all about motors: how to drive, how to strip down an engine and put it back together, how to get into any car in a few seconds, how to make a Slim Jim, how to hotwire, how to make a handbrake turn; all of it. To me, Jake was a god.

Jake was a modder – someone who takes a motor and modifies it for speed or display purposes. He spent every penny he could save from his day job at Jig and Brace and from his extra hours on the ratburger griddle. All of it went on modifying his car, trimming out the interior, tuning up the engine and parading it on cruise nights up on the old Roman road.

In fact, his twocing days were over. He'd graduated to this other scene. The secret word would go out over the Internet and they would be up on the Roman road to race, turn, spin cars and perform pointless tyre burn-outs for each other by holding the car still with the handbrake. Smoke heads. But Jake was a modder for show *and* a modder for go. They would illegally block off the road at two ends to run the modders' sprint at speeds of up to 150 m.p.h.

Jake totalled his RS Cosworth in a sprint. It had been modified up to 600 b.h.p. All the excess petrol in the fuel chamber went up, and Jake was a human torch. They said that when they got his burned body out of the car, his mobile phone, melted to his skin, was still ringing.

That was me calling. I was ringing to find out if he'd won the race.

Jools had been Jake's girlfriend for a very short while. She was a couple of years younger than he was, and a year older than me. Out of my league, I always thought. *Way* out of my league. Luckily for Jools, her parents kept her on a pretty strict curfew, so she wasn't out with Jake the night he died.

She kept in touch with our family. She used to call round to see Mum from time to time. She was sweet like that. Then, one day, completely out of the blue, she mentioned that her birthday was coming up, and she wasn't doing anything. And I remembered that she was a fan of the Lockhearts. And I knew where I could get my hands on some tickets.

Would she go with me? Yes, she'd love to. *Love* to.

It was perfect. I could take her out for her birthday. I could take her for Jake. He'd want it that way. It was destiny, like when you're counting the cars and they all line up in the order of your best times. These things were all lining up. I would take her out for her birthday. I would finish school. We would go out together. I would marry her. I know how stupid that sounds, but that was how I was thinking. And even Jake would approve.

Or maybe this is how things might have lined up, except that the tickets never arrived. That part was also true. Dad did give me some money as well, but to take Jools to the cinema. That wasn't good enough. I wanted to impress Jools by taking her to the wine bar. But there was that barman, the shaved ape who wouldn't serve me. Made me feel stupid. Made me look about *that* small in front of Jools. 'Sorry kid, I'll do you a nice Coke, but nothin' else.'

I could see him looking her over, as if to say, 'Hey pretty girl, what are you doing with that *kid*?'

Everything was going wrong. The evening was coming unglued. We were leaving the wine bar, me cursing the barman under my breath and with my cheeks still flaming, and Jools going, 'Oh, it doesn't matter, we'll go to the cinema,' when the Testarossa, the fatmobile, parks up outside the restaurant.

So I had to show Jools how easy it was to take it.

Because I could.

You know: be the big cheese.

Yep.

Everything else is pretty much true. We went up to the Roman road and I showed her a few handbrake turns and a tyre burn-out. She couldn't stop laughing. I was a prince. We found the skunk in the glove compartment and we smoked ourselves silly. We drove slowly through the tunnel in the dark. Then we found the other burned-out car in the siding. It was spooky. Neither of us could figure out how they'd got it there. I turned off the lights again. She grabbed hold of me in the dark. I knew what it was like to feel wanted.

Then we drove the fatmobile back to the tunnel entrance and sat there for a while in silence. That was when I saw the old guy, the one walking his dog. I think he must have called the police.

I wanted to kiss Jools, but I couldn't bring myself to the point. It was like everything I said and did was magnified. Like I was on stage under a spotlight. Like I was a clown with huge feet. I kept thinking: What would Jake do? What would Jake do? I even heard his voice in my ear saying, 'Just lean over and gently put your lips against hers.' But I couldn't do it.

I saw the patrol car inching down off the road and into the field. They had doused their headlights, trying to be clever, but I still saw them coming. We were going to be caught. The birthday evening was about to end in the police station, with phone calls to my folks and to Jools' mum and dad.

This is the point where I want to blame Jake. I saw the police car in the rear-view mirror of the fatmobile and I froze. Maybe it was the skunk, but in that moment Jake reached over from behind the seats and put a hand on my shoulder. He told me not to panic. Told me he'd taught me how to deal with these situations.

And I had the brainstorm. That's when I figured out how that other car – the burned-out wreck – had got itself in that weird position in the tunnel siding.

'Handbrake turn,' I said.

'You got it,' said Jake.

'What?' said Jools, who at that point wasn't even aware of the patrol car creeping up behind us.

Yeh. Handbrake turn. Obvious. You see, you couldn't turn the car into the siding. There wasn't enough room and the steering lock wouldn't give you clearance. And I wouldn't have had time to stop the car and reverse back up the siding as I'd done earlier, because the police would be right on us.

Maybe it was panic. Maybe it was because I was so stoned. But a million-watt lightbulb went on in my brain and I saw the way to do it in a vision of white light. I saw it clearly as the police car bumped quietly across the field towards us.

I knew that if I could kill my lights and manoeuvre the fatmobile into the siding in the tunnel, the police car following would speed right by us, right to the end of the tunnel, missing the fork just as we had done. I could then reverse out before shooting forward all the way back to the tunnel entrance. Leaving Plod high and dry at the other end.

Perfect.

Yes, I knew how to do it. High speed. Handbrake turn. Skid the back end of the fatmobile to beat the steering lock. A good speed would shove me round nearly 180 degrees, all ready to shoot up into the siding like a fox into a hole. It would work. That's how the other car got up there.

Beautiful.

With the police car crawling towards us over the field, I revved the engine and squirted the fatmobile into the tunnel. Jools went shooting back in her seat. I saw the lights of the police car come on behind me. They were up for the chase. They were going to follow us inside. I booted the accelerator and put my head-lights on full beam.

The fatmobile was crunching stuff under the wheels and at this speed it threatened to hit the side of the tunnel. I saw the 'DOOM' graffiti come up on my side. It flashed past. I was watching the walls, looking for that crucial fork. I had my foot hard down and when we hit the critical point I killed my lights, spun the wheel, jammed on the handbrake and went shrieking into the skid.

It almost worked. It could have worked.

Looking back on it, I figure I miscalculated maybe by only a few inches. The front end of the over-designed fatmobile clipped the wall and turned the car a fraction early. The metal body of the car was grinding against the brick wall, sending out a shower of sparks. The sharp corner at the fork sliced through the rear wing like a can opener. It also opened up the petrol tank. Meanwhile, the windscreen cracked and bits of shattered glass pelted us like a stream of razor blades.

The car rammed hard up against the wall and Jools was thrown across me. Then the spilled petrol ignited. We couldn't get out. The engine was stuck in high revs and I couldn't get the door open. The panel of the door was bashed in and I couldn't get the handle to release. Meanwhile, Jools' passenger door was flush up against the wall. The car was burning and we couldn't get out.

Jools was screaming. One of the policemen ran up and tried to open the door. He couldn't do it. He ran away, only to reappear with a crowbar. Finally, he managed to jemmy the door off its hinges. By this time his hair was on fire. It didn't stop him. He pulled Jools and me out of the car.

I don't remember a single thing after that.

That's it. That's the truth of it. And this is the first time I've told anybody.

25

None of That Girlie ABS

Amy and Gilb look at me with bulging eyes. I see Gilb's Adam's apple roll in his throat as he swallows.

'So,' says Amy. 'No Jake.'

'No Jake.'

'So where did Jake come from?' says Gilb.

Amy answers for me: 'Matt needed him.'

'I don't get it,' says Gilb.

But Amy got it immediately. 'Haven't you ever lied to yourself, Gilb? So you wouldn't have to face up to the truth about something you've done? Especially when there's no one else to blame. I know that I have.'

She was right. I'd blamed Jake because I couldn't stand what I'd done to Jools. He was the last thing I thought of when I panicked in the tunnel and tried to go for the handbrake turn. The thing is, I couldn't get rid of him. 'Jake was there when I woke up in the hospital,' I tell them. 'Now he's with me pretty much all the time.'

'All the time?' asks Amy.

'Oh yeh. I mean, he's here now.'

'Now?'

'Yeh. Right now. Actually, he's been with us since we picked up the Cerbera.'

I nod behind me, at the space behind the seats. Jake is curled up there, looking remarkably relaxed. He's not a coal-miner any more. Now he's a railway stationmaster. He has a peaked cap, a jacket winking with silver railway insignia, and he's holding a ticket punch. 'End of the line,' goes Jake. 'Tickets, please.'

Amy and Gilb can't help themselves. They both crane their necks over the back of the seat, to check it out. Then they both look back at me.

'Why did you tell them that?' says Jake. 'You tosser! You know perfectly well they can't see me.'

'Are you joking?' says Amy.

'Of course I am,' I say. 'Of course I'm joking.'

'Admit it,' says Jake. 'She's funny-looking, but there's something sexy about her. You fancy her, don't you?'

'You know what's the stupidest thing?' says Amy. 'We only had half a day to go. Before we were finished at Arnedale Lodge, I mean. Half a day and we would have earned all our credit points. But we've blown it now.'

'Why did you come with me? I really want to know.'

'Well,' goes Amy, looking at Gilb. 'The truth is we kind of like you. But we would never say that. Isn't that right, Gilb?'

'Yer,' says Gilb. 'We'd never say it.'

'Get rid of them,' says Jake. 'Get on with it.'

I reach across and pop open the passenger door. 'Amy, Gilb, it's been good fun, but I'd like to be left alone now. You can find your own ways home, can't you?'

'What are you going to do?' Amy wants to know.

'Don't tell her,' says Jake.

'Oh, I dunno,' I say. 'I'll just sit here and have a think. Then I'll go home. Face the music. Face the Royal Philharmonic Orchestra with full brass and strings section. You know.'

But that Gilb, as I suspected all along, is not thick. He may watch the world with dead-fish eyes and with his mouth hanging half open, but never let it be said that my new mate Gilb is stupid. 'He's gonna do it all over again.'

'Do what?' says Amy.

'Do it again,' says Gilb. 'In this.'

Now it's Amy's turn not to get it. And I know why. She's not slow. It's because she doesn't *want* to get it. Gilb is right, of course. I don't know how much he knows about motors, but what we have here in this Cerbera is a different proposition to the fatmobile that so badly let me down. Unlike the fatmobile, the Cerbera is almost a racing car, and it has the braking power to match: massive AP racing brakes to drag-stop just as hard and fast as the damn thing can run. Hell, the front discs are the size of an Escort's wheels. None of that girlie ABS lark. It's like having two grappling hooks that come out of the wheels and crack deep into the road. Brakes that do exactly what you tell them, when you tell them. Brakes that will eat the road underneath us. Brakes that will get me round the corner. And after all, I have a point to prove to Jake, don't I?

Jake clacks his ticket punch right under my nose. 'Get on with it. Stop hanging about with these losers.'

'They're not losers, they're my friends,' I tell Jake.

'Who are you talking to?' Gilb wants to know.

The light suddenly dawns on Amy. 'You mean you're going to burn this one, too? In the tunnel? No, you can't.'

'Has to be done,' I tell her.

'You mean it? It wasn't enough, what you did last time? To Jools? To yourself?'

'Hey, fire-starter,' I say, forcing a smile. 'Give me some understanding here.'

But Amy is not smiling. 'I told you. That's in the past. I'm over it. You need to get over it, too. Anyway, we're a team now.' She looks at Gilb. 'Aren't we, Gilb?'

'Yer,' says Gilb. 'Yer. You're stuck with us.'

'Looks like you've got yourself a posse!' says Jake. 'And ain't they pretty!'

I'm trying to ignore Jake. I shake my head. 'No. I'm strictly solo. Now get out of the car and go home.'

'No one is going to pull you out this time, Matt.'

'Right. Just get out.'

Amy opens the passenger door. 'Have it your own way,' she says. She climbs out, as does Gilb. Amy slams the passenger door shut. Then she comes round to my side. I touch the button and the window winds down with a gentle purr. 'I want to give you something before you kill yourself.'

'What's that?'

She puts her face close to mine and plants a gentle kiss on my lips. Her lips stay pressed against mine. Just when I'm thinking how sweet Amy really is inside the tough, streetwise shell, she makes a grab for the ignition wires dangling under the dash. She manages to grab the wire but she's not fast enough. I have her wrist clamped in my hand. She's going nowhere.

'Let go!'

I hold her hand exactly where it is. She knows if she drags the electrical wires out from under the dash that I'm not going to be able to spark the engine up again. If she does that, it's all over.

'Let go of the wires,' I tell her again.

I twist, hard. But she's tough. She holds on. Our eyes lock. I twist harder and I push her fingernails hard back. Her eyes water a little. She's still staring at me. 'I don't want you to do this.'

'Let go, Amy.'

Gilb comes across. 'Look, it's four o'clock in the morning. With this car, we could drive back all the way to Arnedale Lodge before anyone is even awake. Nobody would even know we were gone.'

'Ack ack ack! He's the funny one in the family!' says Jake.

'Gilb, my old mate, I have a point to prove,' I say. 'I didn't ask you two to come with me. And now you're both just getting in my way. Let go of the wires, Amy!'

Suddenly she relaxes her grip. Now that the electrics are safe I let her pull back. She withdraws her head from the car. She just gives up. But as she does so I see her looking at my hands as they grip the steering wheel. My scarred and melted hands. I think of how she kissed my hands in the yak-yak session only yesterday, yet it seems like a lifetime ago.

'What?' I ask her, revving up the engine, tickling the gas.

'Nothing,' she says, turning away. 'Know what, Gilb? He wants to fill his brother's boots. That's what he's doing now. He's always wanted to fill Jake's boots. He wants to go the same way.'

'Enough talk!' Jake shouts at me. 'Do it!'

I toe the accelerator again. The engine pops and crackles, low and throaty. Sweet. Maybe Gilb and Amy see sparks, because they both jump back, away from the car.

Jake swings himself into the passenger seat and winds down the window. 'Let's prove a point,' he says.

Gilb runs up and has a last dig, trying to get me to stop. He puts his hands either side of his mouth, to make a megaphone so I can hear over the popping and crackling of the engine. 'You fucked up!' I think he says. 'You don't need to spin the car. All you need to do is reverse all the way past the fork and then drive straight into the siding.'

This confuses me. I think about it. 'Jake?' I say.

'Ignore that twat!' shouts Jake. 'Get on with it.'

I strap myself in. I notice Jake doesn't bother with his seat-belt.

'Wuss,' says Jake. 'Pussy.'

And then I boot it.

Power unleashed. The Cerbera springs into the tunnel like a panther leaping in the dark. The car is filled with a rush of dank air from the tunnel, streaming in through the open windows. Jake sticks his head out, roaring, urging me on, faster, faster. I'm accelerating into the blackness, with Jake still screaming into the wind. The engine crackles. We hit maybe a brick but the Cerbera absorbs the shock, doesn't waver. My lights are on full beam. We pass the graffiti on the wall: 'DOOM!' It suddenly occurs to me that it might be one of Gilb's. Hell, too late to ask him now. I'm tanking up to the point of no return.

'It's coming up!' shouts Jake, punching the air. 'Whoooooooooo! Any second now!'

That's right. Any second now. My right hand rests lightly on the top of the wheel, ready to whip it round. My left is clutching the handbrake. I know exactly the spot, better than Jake does. After all, he wasn't the one who went a moment too soon last time, before everything ended in fire. Fire is how the world ends. Everyone knows that.

The moment drops into a weird zone, a pocket of slow motion, from where I can see everything super-clear. I see my whole life. Mum. Dad. The day Jake died. Me trying to call him on his mobile while his body is being lifted from his burned-out rig. Gran sitting in her old folks' home staring at the blank TV screen. Jools with her scarred face. All this somehow appears in one perfect, whole picture, exactly like one of Gilb's paintings, with these images shaped inside a giant wheel, maybe a steering wheel. And my hands, my burned hands, are gripping the wheel.

And I know that everything is in my hands.

The point approaches fast where I have to make the spin. I can see it coming. More than that, I can sense the exact moment surging towards me. The hidden siding creates a slight change in the air pressure as it comes rushing up. Jake is screaming, '*Do it! Do it!*' The Cerbera is popping and crackling.

And there's other stuff in my head, too. Voices: Sarah; Pete; Alex; Cookie going, 'His Lordship decided to crash the car!'; Gilb telling me I'd got it all wrong; Amy saying . . .

I hit the brake, hard. Not the handbrake, the footbrake. I keep the wheel still. The Cerbera bites hard at the track underneath. The sound is like the squeal and crunch of hitting a market-fattened herd of pigs. Dead stop. *Ker-am!* The Cerbera stops on a pin, and Jake goes flying out of the passenger window, still roaring.

I hear his bones crack as he hits the wall in the dark.

26

I Love Everybody

No, I don't execute the handbrake turn. I don't spin the wheel. I just rip into the ground with the hottest set of brakes on the planet.

When Jake goes whizzing out of the window, only my seat-belt stops me going through the windscreen. I don't know when or if he'll be back, but I'm not thinking about him any more. I kill the lights, and I sit there in the dark with the engine simmering quietly, thinking. About something else.

Amy and Gilb. I have no idea why they care about me. After all, I've spent most of my time with them behaving like the smart-arse, piss-taking, know-it-all big-mouth I seem to want to be. Why would they even give a damn?

It bothers me, big time. And I think I know why. I think Amy and Gilb know that we're three of a kind. Outsiders, hanging together. Misfits, fitting each other. Three damaged kids, trying to find a way through. Amy and Gilb like it that I'm like them: a bit screwed up. Is that right? Is it possible to like someone even with their faults?

For the first time in my life, I think it is. Maybe. Factoid number seven: even the best people are not perfect. So maybe I don't have to be, either.

After a while I turn on the headlights again, and I slowly reverse out of the tunnel. When I reach the entrance, Gilb and Amy are there waiting with big round eyes, their faces lit up by my white reversing lamps and the red tail-lights. I creep out of the tunnel, stop, and get out. They both come up to me.

The sky is lightening. It's not dawn yet, but the sky is turning that white-grey cotton-wool colour you get beforehand. The air is damp. I can feel the moisture on my cheeks. I feel okay.

'Amy, I love you,' I say.

'Huh?' she goes.

'Gilb, I love you, too. I want you both to know that.'

Gilb gives me that shit-eating sideways grin of his, that keyboard smile. Then he looks at Amy, and I can tell they're both thinking: Time. To. Get. Out. Of. Here. Factoid number seventeen: tell people you love them and that's what they think. Who cares? Amy is looking at me like I'm a lit match falling into a box of fireworks.

'Don't worry,' I say. 'Don't worry about a thing.'

'Did you do it?' asks Gilb.

'The handbrake turn?'

'Yes, the handbrake turn.'

'No. I didn't do the handbrake turn. It was because of what you shouted just before I set off. Thank you for pointing that out.'

'Yer,' he goes. 'Well.'

'How did you figure it out?'

'Obvious,' he says. 'You just reverse back up the tunnel and when you have passed the turn you can drive straight in. Anyone can see that.'

Anyone except me, because I've blinded myself to it. Blinded myself with my fake version of events. Blinded myself because I've been too scared to look at what I've done, and at what I am. Once I heard a story about a boy who was badly injured by a train. He said he'd been seeing how close he could get his head to the tracks before a passing train would hit him. Guess what? He found out. I figure me and that boy are about on the same level.

That's not what I say to Gilb, though. Instead I say, 'You've been here before, haven't you? That graffiti mural in there – one of yours, isn't it? Doom.'

'An early one,' says Gilb. Yeh, like this is his 'early period' of paintings, like Picasso had a 'blue period'. 'They don't count unless there's a risk of being caught.'

I turn to Amy. 'How long?' I ask her.

'Eh?' She's still looking at me like I'm about to go *bang*.

'How long would it take us to get back?'

'We can do it,' says Amy. 'We can still get back before they're awake. If we go right now.'

I walk over to the Cerbera and open the driver's door. 'So what are we waiting for?'

The Cerbera still has half a tank of fuel. We debate which is the more risky route: whether to swing round the back roads hoping once again to miss the patrol cars or whether to save time on the motorway. We weigh it up and choose the motorway. It's the graveyard shift. Even the meanest law-breakers have gone to their cots. The Cerbera could rip up the miles but I stick to the speed limit. We don't see a single patrol car all the way.

Eventually we have to come off the motorway and go in search of the minibus we left outside the village church. We get a little lost, but no one is panicking and we think it through. Both Amy and Gilb are good in a crisis. We work it out.

And there it is, parked right where we left it under the branches of a yew tree. We leave the Cerbera, though in a way it breaks my heart, and climb inside the minibus. The keys are still dangling in the ignition.

'This is going to work!' says Amy, buckling her seat-belt.

'Arnedale Lodge is about fifteen minutes away,' I say confidently. 'Twenty tops.'

We've all got the giggles.

I turn the key in the ignition. Nothing happens. I turn the key again. And again. The battery is completely flat.

27

Jam On It

Nothing doing. Doornail. As in dead as. Pancake-o. Kaput. Flat battery. It's well after dawn, the sun is rising over the treetops, we're going nowhere and now after all this my brain feels as dead as the battery. I bang my head against the steering wheel in frustration.

'Can't you start it?' says Amy. 'I thought you were the expert. Why can't you hotwire it?'

'No,' I say, very patiently. 'To hotwire an engine, the wires have to be hot. For that, you need a charged battery.'

'Oh.'

'Yes: "oh". We'll have to try to bump-start it.'

Easier said than done. To start with, neither Amy nor Gilb knows how to bump-start a car. Kids these days! What the hell do they teach them at school? The minibus is very heavy and we are on a flat road. We need to get up a little momentum to turn over the engine.

Gilb and I being stronger, Amy is going to have to take the driving seat, but she hasn't got a clue. 'I can't do it! I'll crash it!'

'No, you won't,' I tell her, 'I'll put it in gear. You keep the clutch down and when I shout, lift your foot off the pedal.'

'Which one's the clutch?'

'Left pedal, for Christ's sake.'

Reluctantly, Amy climbs into the driver's seat. I lean across her and shift the gearstick into first. Then she wants to know, 'What will happen when I lift my foot?'

'Never mind that. Just give it some gas on the accelerator to keep it going.'

'Accelerator? Which one's that?'

Deep sigh. 'Right pedal.'

'It won't go anywhere, will it?'

'Not if you use the brake and slip it into neutral.'

'Oh shit, I can't do this!'

She's gone to pieces, so she gets out and I climb in the driver's seat in her place. Gilb and Amy push. It's useless: the thing creeps along an inch at a time. I have to bully Amy back into the driving seat and go through it all again with her. 'Jam the brake on if you get scared. Just don't steer it into the ditch.'

Gilb and I lean our backs against the rear of the minibus to get it rolling. Blisters of sweat burst out on my forehead. I'm trying to think how much time we have left before they rise and shine at Arnedale Lodge. Cookie's probably first up, melting a tombstone-size slab of lard into his frying pan.

Gilb and I are heaving and pushing and sweating and I think this is just how it is: one minute I'm in a Cerbera smelling the beautiful new leather upholstery and the whiff of high-octane fuel, powering down the motorway, an aristocrat of the road; the next minute I'm slogging my guts out trying to shove this ugly battery-dead crate for young convicts along a country road. Factoid number forty-two: life can turn on the smallest things.

The minibus starts to roll. Gilb and I turn together like dancers and we push forwards. We get up a bit of speed.

'Now, Amy! Get off the clutch!'

The engine coughs into life and farts a big blue cloud of exhaust right in our faces. The minibus lurches forward. Amy jams on the brake. The engine almost dies.

'Hit the gas!'

Amy revs the thing until it squeals. We must have stirred the whole neighbourhood. These dead people in the churchyard must be awake, poking their heads up through the mossy graves and wiping cobwebs off their faces.

'That's enough gas, Amy!'

Gilb and I run up and fling ourselves inside the moving minibus. I climb in the driver's side and slip my foot on to the accelerator pedal, under Amy's foot. She shoves over into the middle of the seat and lets me take control of the wheel. Gilb is only halfway in the passenger side as we move off. The door swings open and he goes with it, hanging on by his fingertips. It swings back and he's able to scramble safely inside. He's giggling again.

Amy is shaking, really trembling. 'Did I do okay?'

'You did bloody brilliant!' I tell her. 'Give her a kiss, Gilb.'

And Gilb gives her a noisy smacker on her cheek. 'Gerroff,' she goes. But she loves it. I can tell. Yes, she does.

'Arnedale Lodge, next stop,' I say.

Twenty minutes. On the approach to the lodge I switch off the engine so they won't hear us coming and we freewheel down the hill for about two hundred yards. The minibus has just enough momentum to turn it into the driveway and roll it up the slope. I bring it to a stop near where we picked it up, so no one ever need know we've taken it out.

As far as we can tell, no one is awake. We climb out and delicately close the minibus doors behind us. Then we run over to the window where we made our break-out.

The window is a mess. The jam-smeared sheet is there. Glass is still stuck to it. Some shards of glass are on the ground. Gilb climbs back in through the broken window and comes back with the rest of the cut-up sheet. We wrap all of the glass and the jam-smeared cloth in this big sheet. The funny thing is no one has to give orders or tell anyone what to do. We all know instinctively. We're like a well-oiled machine. Amy goes back inside and starts clearing up. Gilb picks any last bits of glass out of the frame. I take the sheet bundle and race across the yard to dump it in one of the big rubbish bins. I even manage to disguise it by sticking it in a plastic bin-liner half filled with garden weeds.

Back in the room we unpack our things and we carefully arrange our beds to look like they've been slept in. The only thing out of place – apart from the pretty glaring fact that Gilb and I have got no glass in our window – is this giant, almost empty jam-pot. I'm about to return it to the kitchen when we hear the sounds of pots and pans slamming about in there.

That's Cookie all right. He's a pot-thrasher. A real kitchen drummer. He's got a stainless-steel orchestra in there. I think it fits in with his idea of the temperamental chef. You know: it takes a special kind of noisy, sensitive, creative personality to burn sausages that black. Anyway, he's up and about, and it means I can't get back with this oversized jam-pot.

The normal routine is for Pete to come and bang on our door at 8 a.m. We don't want him to come and inspect the room, so we agree to present ourselves for breakfast a few minutes before that time. We try to freshen up in the bathroom, but we know that without having slept we all look dog rough. But we try to carry it off.

We get into the breakfast room before Pete arrives. Cookie glowers at us through the serving hatch from the kitchen, from inside his stainless-steel empire. He points a finger. 'You lot siddown!' he shouts.

This is unnaturally aggressive, even for Cookie. No 'Good morning, Your Lordship. You chaps are up early.' Just *siddown*.

He's still glowering through the hatch. 'Think you're clever, don't you? Think you're smart! Well, I'll tell you something for nothing: you're not! And I'll tell you something else for nothing: when Pete gets here, you're in the shit. All of you.' Cookie turns away and bangs a stainless-steel whisk into a stainless-steel bowl. Then he slams a lid on to a container.

But Pete's already arrived. He's heard the last part of Cookie's outburst. 'What's going on?' he wants to know.

Cookie beckons Pete over to the kitchen. 'A word in your shell-like, please, Pete.'

Pete goes into the kitchen. They retreat deeper, to the shelves at the back. Cookie does a lot of talking, repeatedly jabbing a finger in our direction, but we can't hear anything that's being said.

'Don't admit to anything,' says Amy. 'Nothing.'

After a while Pete comes out, followed by Cookie. Pete leans his hands against the table. Cookie takes up his usual stance, arms akimbo, knuckles dug into his hips. 'Come clean,' says Pete.

The three of us look at each other, all innocence.

'Look at 'em,' says Cookie. 'Butter wouldn't melt in their mouths.'

'Out with it,' says Pete.

I shake my head slightly. Amy affects a quizzical expression. Gilb holds out his hands, baffled. I know we're overdoing the theatre, but I can't seem to stop myself playing someone who is playing dumb.

Cookie loses patience. 'You're so bloody clever! Well, let me tell you another thing for nothing: there's not a single knife or fork in this kitchen that could go missing without me knowing about it. I inspect it every morning when I arrive and every evening when I leave. You couldn't move a spot of dust without me knowing about it.'

I still don't know what he's talking about.

It's Gilb who gets it. 'All right,' he says. 'We were hungry.'

'That doesn't give you the right to pilfer food from my kitchen!' goes Cookie. 'Where is it now?'

The penny drops, and I realise he's missing his pot of jam.

'We pretty much finished it,' says Gilb.

Cookie explodes. 'What? A five-pound jar of jam! Finished it? What did you eat with it?'

'Nothing,' says Amy. 'We didn't want to take anything else that we weren't entitled to.'

'What? No bread? No nothing? Just five pounds of jam? What sort of people are you?'

I could see the next question coming. 'We borrowed three spoons from the kitchen. But we didn't want to make any extra work for you so we washed them and carefully put them back exactly where we found them.' I'm not the best of liars. I can't stop my foot tapping as I'm saying this. But it seems to wash with Pete.

'Well, that's responsible behaviour at any rate,' he says.

Cookie's not having that. 'That's not good enough! Prowling around at night! Thieving wherever they like!'

'That's a bit strong,' says Pete.

'They're here to mend their ways, not to practise being light-fingered in the middle of the night! They come here and go horse-riding and what-have-you and they think it's a bloody holiday camp. Well, it's not good enough, and I'm going to have to put it in my report that they've all been thieving and nothing was done about it.'

I can see Pete's in trouble. He knows that Cookie is right, but he's probably thinking that, after all, it's only a pot of jam.

Then Amy pipes up: 'But don't we put a report in, too, Pete?'

'That's right,' says Pete. 'You get to write an evaluation.'

'Well,' says Amy, 'I'm going to have to say that we don't get enough food here, and that's why we took the jam.'

'You get plenty!' roars Cookie.

'But it's not nutritious. And it's not well cooked. And I'm going to have to say we were so hungry, that's why.'

'I'll have to say the same thing in my report,' I say. 'And the food is very badly presented.'

'Burned, often,' says Gilb, 'and I'll have to say that in my evaluation.'

I don't know why, but we've somehow made it sound like we've been appointed as heads of a government inquiry investigating catering at Arnedale Lodge. Cookie is fuming. He's gone quiet. He looks like he's thinking about going back into the kitchen to get some of his big knives.

Pete suddenly becomes Mr Compromise. 'Look, that's not fair to Cookie. He works hard and does a good job with the limited budget available to him. Here's what I think: you should look Cookie in the eye and apologise for invading his workspace and taking the jam. And perhaps Cookie can be persuaded to make no reference to this in his report. And no petty sniping in your evaluations, either. In fact, you might help the situation by suggesting that Cookie should get more resources for catering. That would be more positive wouldn't it, Cookie?'

Cookie's face is red. He grunts and looks at the door.

'So we're all agreed, then?' concludes Pete. 'No mention of the incident, nor any bleating about the quality of the food, and a full-on apology to Cookie right now.'

We all look at Cookie. A bit too quickly, and at exactly the same moment, the three of us say, 'Sorry.'

Cookie turns on his heels and retreats into the kitchen, where he proceeds to give it the crash–bang–wallop bongo-mania on the stainless steel as he prepares breakfast.

Which, incidentally, proves to be every bit as good – and by that I mean gut-rumblingly bad – as it has been at every other serving.

28

Pack Your Own Lunch

Pete has the perfect thing for three kids who have been awake all night. We're going on a hike. A long walk up the hills and through the dales, with heavy packs on our backs. Plus, he's going to show us how to read a map and compass. He calls this orienteering.

Just getting through the morning is enough of a struggle. Just tracking down the brain cell that sends a message to move the foot is quite enough orienteering.

Normally I wouldn't mind that sort of thing. I don't mind a bit of a wander through the countryside. But not when I haven't had a wink of sleep. My eyes keep closing while I'm walking. Whenever I look at Gilb and Amy, they seem to be sleepwalking, too. We just want our beds.

'Eight miles,' says Pete cheerfully. 'Just a short one.'

But we don't want to get rumbled, either. At the moment the only thing we could get caught for is the missing window in our room. And that could lead to suspicions, which could uncover some missing petrol in the minibus, which could . . . I try to stop thinking about it. Anyway, like I say, it's difficult enough to remember to put one foot in front of the other.

We've been given a laminated map of the country-side and a kind of army compass. The needle of the compass is spinning like my head. I feel sick from lack of sleep.

'Look at the contours of the land,' says Pete from the front of our single-file procession over the limestone hills. 'Then you'll be able to locate it on the map.'

'Uh.'

'Mm.'

'Yus.'

'Think I've got three zombies with me today,' quips Pete cheerfully to the sky.

'I'll be honest with you, Pete,' slurs Amy. 'We were up all night.'

'A-ha!' goes Pete. 'Brilliant conversations until the early hours, eh? Well, that's all part of the experience. I've done that in my time. I was young once, too, you know.'

'Umm?'

'Ah.'

'Yus.'

'Oh yes,' trills Pete, 'back in my university days. Staying up all night. Making friends that would last for ever. Putting a bad world to rights. Probably learned more about life from staying up all night than from going to lectures.'

'Duh.'

'Oh.'

'Eh?'

He doesn't seem to want to stop talking as, still in single file, we plod on behind him. He twitters away like a skylark high on all the blue stuff. 'Seeing the dawn come up and wondering how you could have talked an entire night away. Loved it! Of course, you may be knackered now, but you can't burn the candle at both ends. That's one thing I found out. Anyway, you'll learn that yourselves when you all go off to university.'

That wakes me up. 'University? Get real! We're not exactly your university types.'

'Hardly,' says Gilb.

'Ha!' goes Amy. 'Young offenders' institute is more likely for us!'

Pete stops dead. And I mean dead, like the brakes on the Cerbera. *Ker-am!* We all go walking into the back of each other. I get a mouthful of Pete's backpack.

Pete turns on us. 'I'm *not* having that! You do not have to nick cars, burn buildings or paint your way into prison! Anybody can change his or her life! If you *want* to go to university you can fucking well go to university!'

Pete is angry. I don't get it. Nothing has ruffled this guy's calm all week. He's been like a millpond. And now, one word out of place and he's swearing his head off and spitting mad. He's a weird guy, this Pete. He's gone purple in the face. 'Do you understand me? Do you?'

'Sure,' I say.

'And you, Gilb?'

'Err . . . yeh.'

'And you, Amy?'

Amy squints. 'Okay. Yes.'

Pete releases a huge sigh. Then he drops his pack to the ground. Just as suddenly as he went off like a firework, now he's all smiles again. He reaches into his pocket and pulls out his tobacco tin. He rolls himself one of his very thin snouts. 'This would be a good place to study the map,' he says.

We make it back to Arnedale Lodge, barely awake. Pete tells us we have one final yak-yak session before lunch and we all groan. He promises us it's just half an hour to achieve what he calls 'closure' on the programme, then it's lunch in Cookie's five-star eatery before we're driven home.

No one seems to have spotted the broken window while we were away.

The final yak-yak is not too bad, apart from the fact that we're red-eyed and yawning throughout the whole thing. Pete is chipper, bright, upbeat about it all. He tells us how much he has enjoyed our days together, and how we will all get a glowing report, yada-yada. Actually, this gets us credits on our period of probation, so it *does* feel good, and I'll be able to look Sarah in the eye instead of at her legs. It comes as a bit of a shock to me that I haven't thought much about Sarah's legs, nor about Debbie Summerhill nude, nor even about Jools' face, for most of the time I've been at Arnedale Lodge.

Pete picks up on his earlier outburst from when we were out foot-slogging round the dales. 'Look, it's about knowing you can change,' he says again. Then he fixes me with shining eyes that make me feel a bit queasy. 'Some people think that they are stuck in a tunnel, and there's no way they can change direction. But you can! You can always break a hole in the tunnel. Always.'

With all this talk about tunnels I wonder if he's on to me. I wonder if he's talking about life in general or me in particular. Maybe it's because I'm so tired, or maybe it's because his eyes are shining, but for a moment I think I might be inside a dream. But if it is a dream, what's really important is this: no Jake.

For the first time since he died I feel clear of my brother.

Meanwhile, Pete has one more trick up his sleeve before he lets us quit for lunch. 'I want each of you to tell me one thing that you have learned that you will take away with you when you leave.'

'Pack your own lunch,' I say brightly.

'Right,' says Pete. He stands up and walks over to a giant flip chart in the corner. He takes a thick marker pen and he writes, in giant letters:

PACK YOUR OWN LUNCH

'I was only joking,' I say.

Pete ignores me. He tears off the sheet and uses a blob of Blu-tac to post my statement up on the wall.

'Up to you,' says Pete. 'What you learn from life is up to you, and jokes are real things, too. What's yours, Gilb?'

Gilb gives us his computer-nerd smile, coughs behind his hand and then says, 'You can find friends in the strangest places.' Then he colours up.

'I like it!' goes Pete, writing it on a new sheet of paper:

YOU CAN FIND FRIENDS IN THE STRANGEST PLACES

'Amy?'

Amy draws up her knees and tucks them under her chin. She thinks for a moment, then she says, 'The fire is out.'

Pete gasps. He lets the hand with the pen fall to his side. 'Wow. Do you mean that?'

'Yes.'

'Do you want to say what's made you think that?'

'Well . . . just some of the things we've talked about. Some of the things I've seen while I've been here.' She looks at me.

Me and Gilb look at each other, as if to say: what the hell are these two talking about. I wonder if Pete knows things about Amy that we don't. I guess he does.

'Right. Want to say any more about it?'

'No,' says Amy. 'I'll leave it at that.'

'You're the boss,' says Pete. 'You're the one in charge of your own life.' And he writes it up:

THE FIRE IS OUT

It's funny, but when you say something off the cuff, it's just air, isn't it? It's a little puff of air from your mouth, and it's gone. But with Pete writing down things on paper and posting them up on the wall, suddenly it's like they were written by Moses. Maybe these things should be chiselled on great tablets of stone. This thought makes me feel stupid.

'Can I change mine?' I ask.

Pete walks up to my statement, tears it off the wall, screws it up and tosses it in the waste-paper basket. Then he goes back to the board and stands there, marker-pen at the ready. Like he knew I was going to say that all along.

The thing is, as I sit there, trying to think up something clever and worthwhile, with Gilb and Amy turned towards me, my mind goes blank. Like I say, maybe it's the lack of sleep and my brain is dead. No lights come on. It's like Moses and the whole world are holding their breath. Then I start to sweat.

I think Pete sees this look of absence and horror on my face, because he puts down his marker-pen. 'Okay, let's not push it. Let's say you're still working on your slogan, eh, Matt?'

I'm grateful for that. I really am. I've no idea why it's such a big deal in my head, but I'm grateful.

'Lunch,' says Pete.

We do lunch. I'd like to say that Cookie, after our recent exchange of views, has gone out of his way to prepare something tasty and inspiring. You know: the full blue-ribbon treatment. I'd *like* to say that, but I can't. Anyway, we're all too tired even to bitch about the food to each other.

Halfway through the meal, Bone turns up. He makes a big noise, croaking his greetings to all and sundry. He shakes hands with Pete, and Cookie has a lunch ready for him, all plated up with a stainless-steel cover over it to keep in the quality. Bone takes a seat next to us and tears into his burger and chips.

'Have we lost one?' Bone says through a mouthful of chips. 'Didn't I bring four of you?'

We don't know if this is meant to be a joke. No one says anything.

'What have you done to 'em?' Bone shouts to Pete. 'They look done in!'

Pete makes some quip about working us through the night shift.

Cookie brings us a farewell treat for dessert. It's some kind of tiny jelly trifle. That is, it's a cube of green jelly with a single segment of pineapple inside it, and this creation is crowned by a blob of artificial cream. No one else is much interested, so Bone, after finishing off his burger, scoops them up and polishes off all three.

'Come on then, let's be having you,' says Bone, wiping jelly and fake cream from his lips.

Outside, Bone has parked his minibus right next to the window of the bedroom Gilb and I have been sharing. The missing glass is pretty obvious. Pete comes out to say his farewells and to help us with our bags. We keep thinking he's going to notice at the last minute. He insists on solemnly shaking us by the hand and wishing us well and all that crap. Amy, Gilb and I have to look bright and keep talking just to distract his attention away from the window. Hell, it goes on for ever.

'If I think of a slogan,' I shout at Pete, striding round to the other side of the minibus, 'I'll write it on a postcard and send it to you.'

'You do that,' says Pete. 'I'd like that.'

'I'll send you a card, too,' says Amy.

'And I'll send you a painting,' goes Gilb.

Cookie has come out now, and stands in his customary position with his hands on his hips. I can tell Pete is a bit taken aback by all this attention and goodwill.

'I'll send you an email,' I say. 'I can send emails.' *Just don't look at that window, Pete.*

Perhaps we're overdoing it. Bone gets fed up with it all. 'Let's go before someone starts crying,' he says.

Pete closes the door of the minibus and the vehicle moves off. We wave like mad. Pete waves back. Cookie doesn't wave: I can tell he smells a rat. His eyes are narrowed, and though he's trying to stop it, his lip is curling into a sneer. But it's not as if we don't like Pete, who really turned out to be a top bloke. It's just that we don't want him to look at the damn window.

We're just leaving the driveway, waving frantically at Pete, when Cookie notices the missing glass. Guess what? For almost the first time since we arrived, he takes both hands off his hips. He points and says something, but Pete is distracted, waving back at us.

Luckily, it's too late, and we're still waving and Pete is still waving, bye, bye, bye, and Bone toots his horn three times, and the events of Arnedale Lodge are left behind.

(29)

We're Parked on a Meter

I don't remember much of the journey home. Amy and Gilb spark out in the back of the minibus before we've gone two miles. I don't fall asleep immediately because my thoughts are keeping me awake. But I close my eyes and pretend to be asleep so that I don't have to get into a conversation with Bone.

One thing that's keeping me awake is my realisation of what happened before I went into the tunnel. Gilb had seen the easy way, whereas I couldn't. It's a hard thing to swallow: the idea that being smart can make you stupid. And the cleverer you are in your head, the more stupid are the things you can do. My big-cheese plan for evading the police by spinning the fatmobile was stupid.

And the other thing was Amy. Of course, I knew she liked me all along. That's why she cut her hair the way I told her to, even though I was mocking her. I thought if someone likes me – the twocer, the fuck-up, the loser who rearranged Jools' face in the accident, the fast road to hell – well, they must be a basket case. And if you think like that, you end up hating anyone who likes you, like Amy or Gilb, or who loves you, like Mum and Dad.

All that time there was only one person I wanted to be with, and that was Jake. That's why I'd brought him back from the dead. It's while I'm thinking this that I can hear a voice, maybe my own voice inside my head, and it says, 'Pack your own lunch, pack your own lunch,' and I think maybe it's not such a bad slogan after all. Maybe it means 'Don't be content with having someone else shape your life for you,' like Jake did with me, or like I did with Jools. *Pack your own lunch.*

All these thoughts are lurching about in my head, like noisy, crunching changes in the clapped-out gear-box of an old minibus. Then I follow Amy and Gilb into the Land of Nod and drift off to sleep for the rest of the journey home.

The first thing we know about anything is when Bone slides open the doors of the minibus. We all stir, blinking at each other and at the bus station as if staring into strong sunlight, even though the weather is cloudy and overcast. My mum and dad are there waiting, smiling oafishly. Gilb's mother stands with her arms folded, a cigarette on the go. As far as I can see, there's no one there for Amy.

'Don't know what they've been up to,' rasps Bone, 'but they've slept like babies all the way home.'

'Probably better not to ask,' says my mum, laughing chirpily in a way I hate.

We shuffle out of the bus, dragging our bags. My dad dives in and grabs my bag for me. 'You survived, then?' he says.

I blink at him. I don't think he realises how close to the truth he is with this question. Then I understand it's just another way of saying hello.

'How was it?' asks Gilb's mum, stamping out her ciggie on the ground.

'Okay,' says Gilb. 'Good.'

'Some complaints about the food,' says Bone in a comical fake whisper that manages to be just as loud as his normal voice. 'Otherwise, all went well.'

'Good,' says my dad.

'Good,' says Gilb's mum. 'Right then. Better get going. Can't leave the car parked too long.'

'Right then,' says Gilb. He nods at me and then looks at Amy. 'I'll see you around.'

It's like he's waiting for something. Or maybe I'm waiting for something.

Then Amy goes, 'Wait!' She steps over to Gilb and puts her arms round him, and gives him a little hug. Gilb blushes, but he smiles.

'Oh,' goes my mum, 'Isn't that sweeeeeeeeeeet?'

I swear there are times when you could deliver a good, hard karate-chop to your own mother.

'Hey, Gilb,' I say, 'you haven't given me your phone number or anything. I mean, we should meet up.'

Gilb puts his hand in his pocket and brandishes a bit of paper with his number already written on it, as if he'd thought about it already. Then there's a big performance of finding a pen so Amy and I can write down ours. My mum and dad, Gilb's mum and Bone watch this stuff as if it's prime-time television.

When we're done, Bone climbs back into his minibus and starts the engine. He winds down the window. 'Matt, Gilb and Amy, keep your noses clean. I hope I never see you again. And I mean that.' I bet he's cracked this one a hundred times before, but it gets a laugh from my dad at least.

Bone drives off. Gilb walks away with his mother to find their car.

My Dad looks at Amy. 'Can I give you a lift somewhere?'

'No, I'm all right. Thanks.'

'You sure?'

'Yeh, I'm okay,' says Amy.

'How are you getting home?'

'I'll get a bus.'

'No you won't, I'll give you a lift.'

'No good arguing with my dad,' I say.

Dad makes a grab for Amy's bag. 'Come on, we can't stand here arguing. I'm parked on a meter.'

Halfway to Amy's place, Mum asks Amy one of those 'mum' questions, the ones that sound innocent but never are. 'Will there be anyone in when you get home, Amy?'

'Don't know,' says Amy. 'Might be.'

I know what my mum is thinking, though she's probably not too pleased when I say, 'Mum, the food was so bad where we were. Do you think Amy could come back for a bite to eat?'

'No, I'm all right,' says Amy.

'Course she can,' says Dad.

'Honestly,' says Amy, 'I'm fine.'

'It's no good arguing with my dad,' I say again. 'He's a dictator.'

'Shut up, or we'll send you back where you've just come from,' Dad says. But it's all settled.

Amy eats lunch with us at home. I can tell that Mum is bothered by the sixty-four-million-dollar question: what did you do to deserve a holiday courtesy of the probation service? But she doesn't ask. Mum and Dad grill us about the place and what happened there, and we give them horses, caves and compasses.

'Well,' says Mum, clearing away the dishes. 'Looks like you've each made yourselves some new friends.'

Only I can hear the tone of voice that says she'd rather I'd met my new friends at the church youth club. I know that when Amy has gone I'm going to have to defend her to Mum.

After lunch, I show Amy all the kit in my room. She goes a bit quiet. She waves an arm at the PlayStation and the computer and the music equipment. 'And all I've got is a mattress on the floor.' It's like she's saying: 'I've got my excuse. What's yours?'

'You can have it. Any of it,' I say.

'Really?'

'Yeh.'

She looks round the Aladdin's cave of equipment. Then she goes, 'Nah. Don't need it.'

Whatever is at home for Amy, she's in no hurry to get there. She arranges some cushions on the floor and lies down. I sit on the bed and we talk easily. Within a few minutes we're both asleep again.

It's early evening when Mum wakes us with coffees on a tray. 'Don't you think Amy should be getting back? Your dad is getting the car ready.'

The thing is, I don't want Amy to go, and not just because she saved me from myself. Yeh. Ol' Haircut-of-death. I like being near her. I like being around her.

'Oh,' says Mum, before leaving us with the coffee, 'here's your phone.'

Funny, you'd think you'd miss it like a limb, but I hadn't even thought about it after the first night at Arnedale. I switch it on. After a few moments it bleeps.

I don't believe it. There's a text message from Jools. It reads: 'Y u stop texting me'.

'What is it?' Amy wants to know.

I explain the whole thing. She listens carefully. 'What do you want to do?'

You hear that? She doesn't *tell* me what I should do. She asks me what I *want* to do. The truth is, I don't know yet. But the fact that she listens, and then asks me, means that I'm going to ask her for an opinion.

'Come on,' she says, dragging herself to her feet. 'We should get going. Your dad is waiting.'

30

There's Always a Price

I'm at school a couple of days later. English. Mr Butt is creeping round the class, gently prising people's arms aside from shielding their exercise books, breathing his morning-coffee breath over their work, insisting on that eye-contact thing. Actually, I like Butt, when it comes down to it, and I'm doing pretty well in English again.

Plus, I'm sitting behind Debbie Summerhill, entertaining the usual fantasies. I've taken to borrowing stuff from her: pencils, rulers, all things I already have. I can't seem to get myself to do more than grunt by way of thanks, but at least that quacking voice has gone whenever I try to speak to her. One of these days, I'm actually going to ask her out.

I'm just about to tap her on the shoulder and ask for her ruler when a kid from another class comes into the room and speaks quietly to Butt. I hear my name mentioned.

'Matt, it seems you're wanted in the Headmaster's room.'

Everyone in the class turns to look at me. No one gets summoned to the Headmaster's room unless they've done something seriously wrong or somebody has dropped dead. I have a bad feeling in my stomach. I'm rooted to my chair.

'Off you go then, Matt,' says Butt.

It's a long walk down the corridor, past several classes of kids all busy with their schoolwork or at least pretending to listen. Some of the teachers glance at me through the windows of their classrooms as I pass. To get to the Headmaster's study I have to pass through an office where his secretary works. The Headmaster isn't in his study. He's going through some columns of figures with his secretary. He looks at me across the top of his spectacles, and without a single word he points the way through to his study.

I go through, expecting the Headmaster to follow me, but someone closes the study door behind me. The door clicks shut. A man with his back to me is looking out of the window. He wears a long leather coat.

The man turns to me and I see that it's Pete. My heart freezes.

It's all wrong, you see, all out of place. The probation service and the school never cross over like this. I mean, sure, the school knows about my probation record, but they never mention it to me. Ever. It's like two different worlds colliding. It's like a bad dream. It's like a visit from a dead brother.

'Matt,' says Pete. 'Take a seat. Your headmaster kindly allowed me to use his office.'

I sit.

Pete lowers himself into the Headmaster's chair behind this huge desk supporting framed pictures of the Head's family and nothing else. Pete runs his fingers along the edge of the desk in front of him, as if trying it all out for size, feeling what it would be like to be a headmaster instead of a probation officer. 'We need to have a chat,' says Pete.

A chat. I hate chats.

I try to look baffled, as if I've no idea what this is all about, but I already know that it's useless. I swallow, and the sound of my swallowing seems to echo all round the room. 'The window,' I say.

'Yep,' says Pete.

'I'll pay for it,' I say.

'You certainly will,' says Pete.

Then he does that thing of staring at me in complete silence. I look away, then I look back at him. Because I know that if I look away, if I avoid his gaze, it will be worse for me. It's what he wants: eye contact. I feel my face reddening. He hardly seems to blink. This silence goes on for ever. Finally I can't help it. I say, 'What?'

'*What?*' says Pete.

'I just said, "What?"' I say.

'I know you said, "What?" And I said, "What?" back to you.'

I don't know where it comes from, but a bead of sweat rolls down the side of my face. It's like I'm sitting under a supercharged, megawatt interrogation lamp, but all he's doing is looking at me. He's a bastard, that Pete.

'What?' he says again.

I wipe the palms of my hands on my trousers. 'What will you do?'

'Dunno,' he says, and then he starts picking his nails, all casual. 'What do you think I should do?'

'Don't know,' I say.

He loses interest in his fingernails. 'Here's how it runs,' he says. 'I kept thinking about that window and why it would get broken if you weren't going any-where. Then I noticed that the fuel gauge in the minibus was almost on empty, and I could have sworn there was more than that in the tank when I left it after the caving trip.

'Then I did a rough calculation. I got on the blower to two or three colleagues in neighbouring towns. "Any twocing incidents?" I asked them. Well, blow me if a Lexus hadn't been nicked in Ashbourne, and found in Kirby Muxloe. And then an Audi, dumped in Market Harborough. And then a Cerbera, brought back to Ashbourne. A marvellous coincidence. Or a mysterious circle.

'Now those Ashbourne bobbies know plenty of twocers, so they know whose doors to knock, but what surprised them was that the twocers known to them always torch the vehicles so as to leave no evidence behind. No, they thought, this looks more like the work of professionals, stealing to order.'

'*Professionals?*' I croak.

'Yes, that's what the police said. But what they could-n't figure out was what they were after. They didn't seem to take anything . . . much.' Here Pete makes a big fuss of rooting through the pockets of his leather coat. After a lot of huffing and puffing he finds a packet of sweets. He takes one from the packet, tosses it in the air and catches it in his mouth. Then he slides the packet across the desk. I see that they are Mint Imperials. 'Want one?' he says.

'No, I don't like mints . . . much.'

'Really? I'm very fond of a Mint Imperial myself. Very fond.' He gathers up the packet and stuffs it back in his pocket. Then he crunches the mint in his mouth, chews it comically as if it's tough as a bone and looks hard at me.

'What?' I say.

'Oh, don't start that again,' he says, 'for Christ's sake.'

'Sorry.'

'Matt, I want you to understand that I'm here *off the record*. Do you know what that means? It's why I dropped in on your school. I haven't said anything to Sarah or anyone else. So far.' He taps the table in time to these last two words, and says it again: '*So far*. But I know. And now you know I know.'

I open my mouth to say something but he holds up the palm of his hand to stop me. 'No, Matt, you're a good talker but a lousy listener. This is one of those times when you've got to learn to shut your mouth, keep your ears open and walk out of this room a wiser young man. If you *ever* put a single foot out of line again – correction, I don't mean a foot, I mean a toe; no, another correction, I mean a toe*nail*. If you ever put a toenail out of line again, I will use this information against you, and next time you are stuck in a cave with the water rising I will make sure you are left there. Understood?'

I nod. I do understand. And I know he's talking about something that might be even worse than being stuck in a flooded cave.

'Good,' he says. 'Now go back to your classroom.'

I get up to leave. I reach for the door handle but he calls me back.

'Oh, we're forgetting something.'

I turn round and he's reaching across the table with a sealed envelope in his hand.

'What's this?' I ask, taking the envelope.

'It's a bill, which you must pay promptly, for replacing one window, one bedsheet, one pot of jam and one packet of Imperial Mints. Now piss off.'

31

The Coolest Thing

It would be such a relief, I can tell you, if only Sarah would shave her legs. You would think it would be easy, wouldn't you? If I can imagine Sarah nude, why can't I imagine her legs without any hair? But no. In my mind she is butt-naked and yet you could make a Guardsman's hat out of the furry stuff on her legs.

'So,' says Sarah. 'Our last meeting.'

I twitch her a smile. Not that I want to look too pleased with myself. 'Yeh.'

'Well, you've made good progress.' She frowns at her notes. 'Good progress.'

And I have, I suppose. After Pete's surprise visit to school, I told Mr Butt, Ol' Coffee-breath, that I really wanted to make a go of it. He's helping me catch up. After a lot of stiffness and difficulty I can hold a pen properly in my burned hand. I have to grip it in an odd position, but I can write just as well as I did before.

I've started to sit next to Debbie Summerhill.

I get a lot of stick about that from Druce and the others, but I've decided I'd rather sit next to someone sexy and gorgeous than mess around at the back of the class making todger jokes and looking thick. And anyway, there's another reason for me wanting to do well at school.

I've made a pact.

I've made a pact with Amy. We hang around together now. She comes round to my house quite a lot. She's always been really bad at school, but I'm helping her and she catches on fast. She was one of those people who think they're scoring a point over their teachers by pretending to be thick. But she's one of the secretly smart people. She's been hiding it. We're going to trick them. We're going to spring it on them just how smart she is.

Then there's Gilb. He's not so interested in school, and, hell, you can't twist someone's arm. But anyway, we got him to do a painting on a bedsheet instead of on a wall, and Amy and I took it to an art gallery. The guy there was impressed. He's trying to get something going for Gilb. But the guy says he wants Gilb to 'retire' from graffiti art. Sixteen and already retired. How mad is that? Gilb says he's working on one last piece and then he'll quit. I'll believe it when I see it. The Gilbs of this world never quit.

We paid the bill for the window between the three of us. Well, mainly Gilb and I paid it since Amy doesn't have a penny to her name. We sold a lot of stuff, like CDs and video games and some of my computer equipment.

And my days on probation are at an end. I've been a lot more open with Sarah about things, so when she asks me the tricky questions I can deal with them.

'So,' she says, 'no more visits from you-know-who?'

'From Jake?' I say. 'No, he hasn't been back.'

It's true. I haven't seen him since he shot out of the Cerbera window in the Pikehorn Tunnel. Maybe that's where he'll stay, haunting the tunnel, scaring the crap out of kids who venture inside. As for me, I've got no plans to head back that way.

I decide to tell Sarah my other bit of information. 'Oh, by the way, I saw Jools.'

For a minute Sarah doesn't seem to know who I mean. Then the penny drops. 'Jools? You've been to meet her? Really?'

'Yeh.'

I'd told Sarah that we'd exchanged a few messages. After I got back from Arnedale Lodge the texts progressed to emails. I have to say that some of the emails were pretty angry. After a while I asked her if I could see her, and to my surprise she said yes. I talked about it with Amy. It was Amy who said I should just let Jools say what she had to say and not try to fight back or defend myself, and that's what I did.

'Well? How did it go?' asks Sarah.

'Pretty rough. She said some things.'

'Whatever she said, you deserved it.'

'I know.'

'How did she look?'

'Pretty bad.'

'Bad, eh?'

'Yeh. Bad.' What can I tell Sarah? I mean, bad is bad. I'm not going to say: 'Well, if she uses a lot of make-up it might look okay if the lighting is dim.' I just won't say that. The truth is, I would push my own face into broken glass if it would bring back Jools' good looks. But it won't. 'If I could take it away from her and put it on myself, I would.'

'I believe you, Matt. It's one of the hardest things to learn: that everything you do has a consequence for yourself *and* for the people around you. And very often you can't just put things right afterwards.'

I nod in agreement, but secretly I'm thinking, Tell me something I don't know. I know I won't be seeing Jake's face again, but Jools' face will always be with me.

Then Sarah crosses her hairy legs, and I wince. Seeing the expression of pain on my face, Sarah asks, 'Are you all right?'

'Yeh. I'm fine.'

Sarah signs me off, and I'm free. Free of the probation service, free of Sarah's hairy legs, free of Jake. I'm not planning to go back. Amy and Gilb are waiting for me outside. They have also been signed off, and we're going to celebrate.

We're going to steal a car, graffiti-art a bank and burn down a shopping mall.

Just kidding.

'Finished?' asks Amy. She and Gilb are sitting on a low wall outside the probation service building.

'Done,' I say.

'Come on then,' she says. 'Gilb has got something to show you.'

Gilb grins at me. He looks pretty pleased with himself. 'What is it?'

'Follow me.' Gilb slouches off down the street. He digs his hands so far into his pockets he's nearly pulling down his pants. We fall in with him. Gilb leads us to a small, secluded pay-and-display car park. At one end of the car park is a concrete wall. Gilb has brought us here to show us his 'retirement' project.

It's beautiful. He must have used stepladders or something, because it's nine feet high and about twenty-five feet across. And I recognise the brick-work and the yawning mouth of the Pikehorn Tunnel immediately. I'm in it, Amy is in it and Gilb is in it, but it's all swirly and distorted, not like a real-life painting. Gilb has painted himself in the corner, as a figure with a spray-can in his hand, still finishing the painting. I'm driving a sporty car, like the Cerbera but with an open top. The car is spitting out flame from its exhaust, and the mouth of the tunnel is like the gates of hell. Then there's Amy. She's flying. She has wings, like an angel. She's swooping in and lifting me from my seat. Gilb has stencilled two slogans over the painting: 'THE FIRE IS OUT'; 'PACK YOUR OWN LUNCH'.

'Good, eh?' says Amy. She's obviously seen it earlier.

Good? I'm choked. I almost feel like crying, but I don't know why.

'It's a present,' says Gilb. 'For both of you.'

Amy says, 'Come on, let's go. What are we going to do to celebrate our finishing probation, Matt?'

Before I have time to answer a silver-grey Porsche 911 Turbo S pulls into the car park, growling low as its driver cruises into a bay. My heart goes pitter-patter. The driver gets out, collects a ticket, locks his car and shoots us a look before leaving the car park.

'We could take that for a little spin,' I suggest.

Gilb flashes me one of his sideways grins. 'Cool,' he says.

'Yeh, cool,' says Amy, flaring her eyes at me.

But by now they know me so well that they know I'm joking. I'm done with all that. We're not going to touch the Porsche. They don't have to say anything as we walk out of the car park. Yet it makes me laugh. Because, against all the odds, both of them turned out to be pretty cool.